Home Theatre

Home Theatre

Anthony Lapwood

TE HERENGA WAKA
UNIVERSITY PRESS

Te Herenga Waka University Press
Victoria University of Wellington
PO Box 600, Wellington
New Zealand
teherengawakapress.co.nz

Te Herenga Waka University Press
was formerly Victoria University Press

ISBN 9781776920044

A catalogue record is available from the
National Library of New Zealand

Published with the assistance of a grant from

ARTS COUNCIL OF NEW ZEALAND TOI AOTEAROA

Printed in Singapore by Markono Pte Ltd

'I thought of a maze of mazes, of a sinuous, ever growing maze which would take in both past and future and would somehow involve the stars.'
　　—Jorge Luis Borges, 'The Garden of Forking Paths'

'Space however can become a place when filled with things spoken of earlier, such as: Cultural practices, things, values and of course people.'
　　—Wikipedia, 'Community of Place'

'The main interest in life and work is to become someone else that you were not in the beginning. The game is worthwhile insofar as we don't know what will be the end.'
　　—Michel Foucault, in interview

'So even in a book, as in life, closure is an artifice.'
　　—James Gleick, *Time Travel: A History*

'All writing is in fact cut-ups. A collage of words read heard overheard. What else?'
　　—William S. Burroughs, 'The Cut-Up Method of Brion Gysin'

Contents

The Source of Lightning

The lightning above the city reminded me of home. As a kid, I used to watch through the window of my attic bedroom as those immense electrostatic veins bared themselves against the clouds. The roofs of the houses in their expansive topography of ridges and valleys would become etched in flashes of silver. Then that brief image of the world would dissolve as the lightning withdrew. With each new pulse of light, the world would look different, would be somehow reconfigured. Those nights seemed to promise many worlds hidden somewhere inside the one world I knew by day.

My kid-brain couldn't have imagined the truth of that notion, even as a loose metaphor. Nor could I have imagined that years later I would enter an older iteration of the world on a lightning strike—of a kind. Branching through the layered cosmos, propelled through a slipstream in time–space, a tributary of the multiverse. It was a jagged journey as bright and fast and violently alive as lightning.

Hence the advice never to time-travel on a full stomach.

Watching the storm from the living room of my apartment, I thought of the banner at mission control, the scrap of canvas stretched between two wooden posts: GOOD LUCK on one side, WELCOME HOME on the other. On most occasions, there would scarcely be a moment to flip the banner around before the latest agent, departed only a few seconds earlier, would return home from the deep past, exhausted and bursting with knowledge. That could still be me, I thought—I'm not done for yet. I pictured the mission commander hunched over and the 2IC opposite her, each with a four-by-four post in their grip, as I came stumbling back into their present. They'd grin expectantly at me, oblivious to my years stranded in another time because of— well, my bet was a *gravitational wobble* that had disrupted the time machine's trace signal back to home.

Hiccups can happen. They tell us reconnaissance agents not to sweat them—they're unlikely. But should a hiccup eventuate, they also train us in how to run diagnostics and determine a fix. Still, access to the esoteric expertise of the cosmologists and chronotech toolheads at mission control would certainly have boosted my confidence in the diagnosis I'd made and the fix I'd determined to apply. I thought that if I did manage to return to home time, I'd simply be relieved I hadn't blown myself into atomic dust or flung myself into some far-off continuity where salamanders rule the earth.

The thunderstorm gave me hope.

Seeing those blue electric lights arcing, I was reminded that lightning travels in both directions. That it flies not only downwards from the sky but also upwards from the earth. And that despite the old saw, lightning will strike wherever it can, as long as the conditions allow.

It was Wednesday, 06.12.2006. As a simple test that my fix for the time machine had worked, I hoped to leapfrog over the following day, taking me into 08.12.2006.

*
**

A two-step sanity check is recommended when things appear to have gone wrong. Step one: check a clock, a newspaper, anything proclaiming the current date. Step two: seek consensus with another human being.

Thus, next morning at the café, with a nervous sweat already on full display, I enquired about the date when I reached the counter.

The barista told me.

'You're absolutely sure?'

'All day long,' the barista said. 'Christmas is just around the corner, eh. So, what'll it be? Mate, whaddaya after?'

'Long black,' I said, finally.

'Roll the dice, doubles for a freebie . . . Well. That's three-fifty, ta.'

'Why am I back here?' I murmured.

'The coffee's exceptional,' the barista said.

I paid, then sidestepped my way through the crowd to an empty seat in the corner of the café. The crowd's composition, the rhythms and amplitude of the conversation, the handful of distinguishable phrases, were all distressingly familiar. At the front of the café, a woman riffled through the muddled pile of complimentary newspapers. She wore a white T-shirt and denim overalls. I'd stood behind this woman in the queue, that day and the day before. I'd watched as she'd ordered a soy latte, rolled the dice and paid with a fifty-dollar note. That day and the day before, the barista had taken her money and made a show of digging through the till for the right change. He'd sighed and dumped a small pile of notes and coins onto the counter, and she'd swept them, with a reciprocal sigh, into her shoulder bag. That day and the day before, these exact same, ordinary things had happened.

'Long black? Excuse me, long black? This you?'

'Yes, me,' I said to the waitress. My chest felt tight. 'Sorry, can I please get that to take away?'

Back in my apartment's kitchen, I removed the time machine from the over-sink cupboard and withdrew the core from its metal casing. On the core's display, the signatures were tracking nicely, stable as anything. The long-range tether connecting the time machine to the chronochips flowing through my circulatory system was unbroken—the blue indicator at the base of the machine glowed steadily. If the time machine was detecting no abnormalities, then the fault lay in the way I'd reprogrammed it.

The tightness in my chest worsened. I needed fresh air.

Avoiding the building's ancient, lurching lift, I took the stairs, feeling woozy as I spiralled down and exited to the uncovered car park. I doubled over, hands on my thighs, drawing long slow breaths until the tightness eased. Across the car park, in the corner near the skip, a drifter was standing with his head down, searching the asphalt. There were people in the apartment building, busybodies, who would take issue with a person like him hanging around. But he had my sympathies.

Once I was able to breathe and think a little more clearly, I returned to my apartment. I wasn't sure exactly what was going on, but several scenarios seemed plausible. The least offensive was that the day had been reset but linear time would, from that point, continue marching onwards. Of course, only time would tell. I lay on the couch, the curtains closed and the television on, and waited.

*
**

I passed out shortly before midnight and awoke in the morning to find that, once again, it was Wednesday, 06.12.2006.

I repeated the two-step sanity check.

'You're absolutely sure?' I said to the barista.

'All day long,' the barista said. 'Christmas is just around the corner, eh. So, what'll it be? Mate, whaddaya after?'

'Long black.'

'Roll the dice, doubles for a freebie . . . Well. That's three-fifty, ta.'

'I'll get that to take away, please.'

All day long. I examined the ratty pages of my notebooks, hoping to pinpoint the error in the thousands of calculations I'd hashed out in the five years since my return trip by SOP had failed thanks to my hypothesised gravitational wobble. What had I missed in my reprogramming of the time machine that had now thrown me into a loop? I began at the beginning, with notebook 01.01. By evening I'd scoured less than a quarter of one shelf of notebooks, with dozens more shelves remaining, and had filled a further thirty pages with fresh notes, questions, revised formulae, my hands and forearms smeared with ink, growing all the while no closer to locating the critical error, let alone formulating a solution.

At six o'clock, I turned on the television and flipped through the channels. News anchors delivered commentaries as recognisable as the video montages they intoned over. These were, they stated—staring straight down the camera between montages, eyeballing me, insisting on the currency of their coverage—the top stories for today, the sixth of December.

'Has summer really arrived?' asked a newsreader, a man who was fond of reckless, parochial opinions. 'A nasty weather bomb is poised to strike the country's capital this evening. Here's Caroline with the details—' At that moment, however, I loathed him simply for reminding me that I'd made a horrifying mistake that I might well be incapable of remedying.

*
**

Mission rules forbid *the formation of close interpersonal ties in the local temporality*. On the other hand, I was meant to return home upon fulfilment of my reconnaissance objectives, rather than spend five years disconnected and stranded in time, facing the appalling possibility of never returning home at all.

I phoned Ashton.

He worked at the Carter Observatory as an assistant astronomer, delivering live narration for the observatory's planetarium shows, affably assisting families in the learning centre, and herding crowds and answering questions on stargazing evenings. He was a person who liked to help other people.

The observatory was the one place that reminded me of home—the part of home that I thought of with any fondness—with its resemblance to mission control. A resemblance in spirit, I mean, not in its technical capabilities. I'd go there to soak up the familiar atmosphere.

Then, one afternoon, Ashton had tapped me on the shoulder.

'You're a real fan of this place,' he'd said. 'What's the draw, if I may ask?'

More so than any of the other observatory staff, Ashton reminded me of the chronodorks I was closest to back home. Perhaps for that reason, I found myself replying with a degree of sincerity.

'I want to get up there,' I said.

'The roof?'

'No, the stars.'

'Don't we all, my friend.' He paused, weighing something in his mind. 'I could probably swing a private viewing in the telescope room sometime, if you'd like? You're a good customer.'

Watching the night sky together, sometimes smoking weed, shooting the breeze, became a way to unwind. We only hung out at the observatory, and only infrequently. These restrictions helped, I felt, to manage the complications that the mission rules were designed to circumvent, while allowing me to establish some kind of human connection.

On the phone, I cut to the point.

'Have you been experiencing any heavy déjà vu lately?'

'Oh, you know,' Ashton said. 'The same old same old, day in day out, if that counts. Just a sec, I need to find a quiet spot. There are kids everywhere.'

'I mean, do you get the feeling that each day might somehow be exactly the same as the day before—minute for minute?'

'Sure, of course! But I like to mix things up. I like to skip the ham now and then, put a little pastrami on my sammies.'

'There's always pastrami,' I said.

It was good to talk. Ashton all but confirmed I was alone in my experience of an endless, cyclical reality—but knowing he was there, on the other end of the line, lessened my deep unease, if only for the moment.

'They say there's a storm coming,' he said, and then his soft voice softened further. 'Stargazing will be cancelled tonight. I'll be knocking off early, if you want to relax a bit, talk, you know? It gets pretty wild up here on the hill during a storm.'

'Relax a bit' was Ashton's way of saying he'd scored. His colleagues likely knew he smoked, but he had to play the game. I was sometimes tempted to inform him that in the distant future, anaesthetising drugs are about the only thing they allow the populace to consume freely. No stoner ever fought back too hard when the overseers came knocking.

'Got a few things to sort out,' I said. 'Maybe tomorrow.'

'Right. Maybe tomorrow, my friend.'

I hung up.

Ashton's tomorrow would not be my tomorrow. He would climb into bed that night expecting that tomorrow would be different, that a new day would arrive punctually at midnight, unaware that a new day would simply never come.

That evening I watched again through the living-room window as the dark clouds piled thickly above the city and the downpour began. I let the sound and fury of the lightning storm overtake me, thinking blankly of tomorrow and tomorrow and tomorrow.

*
**

It was in the second week of the looping that I saw the drifter again. I'd just left the café and was walking along the block back to the apartment building with my takeaway coffee (still no doubles, no freebie, no surprises). I nearly dropped my cup when I noticed him.

He gave the impression of being formed of a cloud of dense dust, as if a strong breeze would disperse him. He wore the same filthy white corduroy pants and loose grey business shirt as when he'd been lurking around the skip in the car park that first day of the looping. Up close, the drifter resembled my father, from the few old photographs that existed of him, in his early thirties. Most men look that way in the future, and the women too—furtive and thin and unhealthy. An uncertainty hangs over them, about what it means to survive, to propagate, to bring children into a world of so little security.

The years were harder on my father than on me. He and my mother died young, even for their time, in their forties. The academy offered me protections that my parents never enjoyed. Even so, people always said I was my father's spitting image.

But I realised as the drifter drew nearer that, even more than my father, this man on the street resembled me, and I resembled him.

'Change? Coins? Change?' the drifter asked.

His eyes had the milky opacity of advancing cataracts, and he gave no sign of recognition as he approached.

'Change?' he repeated.

I looked into his face and saw my own features reflected back, overlaid with the details of a life weathered differently. Those milky eyes, cheeks rough with stubble, deep lines mapped across his grey, depleted skin. He was the manifestation of a grave threat regarding my own fate. I became immobilised, a hydraulic machine with the fluid let out.

After a moment, I managed to dig into my pocket and draw out a tenner and half a dozen coins.

'Here,' I said. 'All yours.'

He gave a small nod of thanks. He tipped the coins into a pocket of his pants but the note caught in a breeze and fluttered away.

The drifter ambled past me.

I let a dozen metres accumulate between us, then I matched his slow pace. He paused every so often to inspect the ground, and once to ask another passer-by for change. Soon enough, he stopped and looked back over his shoulder, as far as his stiff neck would allow.

'Spaceman,' I heard him say. Then, louder, 'Chrononaut!'

I quickly covered the ground between us and caught his arm. He looked sideways at me, his mouth open and eyes wide. As I began to speak, he tore his arm free of my grip and stumbled off the pavement. I shouted after him and reached out, my fingers seizing for a moment the back of his threadbare shirt as he went onto the road. I felt him pull away as an electric-blue Commodore braked and struck him. His body went limp. He slapped against the bonnet then bounced off and crumpled onto the chipseal surface of the road.

I crouched beside him. The traffic had come to a standstill. I heard someone open the door of the car and a man ask if everyone inside was all right. Another voice, a woman's, was requesting an ambulance.

'I'm sorry,' I said. 'Good grief, I'm sorry.'

He appeared to be unconscious. Raw abrasions mottled the forearm that had broken his fall, and his face was already swelling on the right side, where it had connected with the body of the car. He bled from a cut on his cheek.

His eyes opened.

'Chrononaut,' he murmured. 'Spaceman.'

He rolled onto his side, pushed himself onto his knees, and paused as if praying. Then he stood, turned his face to the sky and pointed at the sun.

'Shadow!' he shouted.

Then he carried on across the road.

'Out of the way,' a woman said, shoving me aside. I looked up and saw it was the customer from the café, wearing her usual white T-shirt and denim overalls. A car ducked around the Commodore and cut off the path between her and the drifter, who was already making his way down the street opposite the café. The traffic picked up. Somebody gave a short blast on their horn and the Commodore rejoined the steady flow of vehicles as the woman retreated to the pavement, shaking her head.

*
**

I kept rolling the dice. You never know.

'Well. That's three-fifty, ta.'

I paid the barista, then took my seat in the corner and watched the café's customers—creatures in a cosmopolitan menagerie—perform their various public morning rituals.

My beard itched. I absently ran my fingers through the rough bristles, probing at my jawline. I had decided I'd pick up a razor on the seventh of December and then off it would come—a ceremonial act. Until then, the beard would provide about the only assurance that I wasn't entirely delusional. That I was in body and in mind progressing along in time, even if the rest of the world was not.

The barista had stared quizzically at the hair on my face as he'd taken my order. Just as he'd done so yesterday, and the handful of other yesterdays before. Each time, in his own recollection of yesterday, I was as blandly smooth-faced as ever.

The waitress seemed not to quite recognise me.

'Long black? Excuse me, long black? This you?'

'Yes, me,' I said.

It still felt extraordinary to expect his reappearance, though it was consistent with everything I knew. I'd watched the drifter pass by the café each day since the car accident—the day I stopped shaving. His gaunt figure soon came into view, framed by the café's front window. I didn't want to cause another scene, but I couldn't simply watch him walk on by any longer. I grabbed my takeaway cup and in my rush to exit I knocked elbows with the woman in the T-shirt and overalls. She spilled soy latte down her front.

'Watch it,' she snapped.

'Sorry,' I said, adding on reflex, 'See you tomorrow.'

'Whatever, dick!'

Ahead, the drifter was nearing the driveway that led to the car park at the rear of the apartment building. I allowed him time to venture up the driveway, then I followed as far as the rear corner of the building, hugging tight to the wall. He headed towards the skip at the edge of the car park. His hands were stuffed into the pockets of his pants and he placed greater weight on one leg. He passed out of view behind the skip's bulk. Keeping close to the wall, I stepped towards the recessed entrance to the internal stairwell at the building's far end, almost opposite the skip. In that shallow hideout I waited some minutes, before the drifter reappeared and made his way back through the car park, down the driveway.

Nothing more than moss and broken glass decorated the asphalt around the skip. I circled it twice before spotting the loose cinder block in the boundary wall. I dragged the cinder block free and laid it on the ground. A cavity had been dug into the earth behind it, large enough to accommodate more than the couple of plastic shopping bags I felt when I reached inside. I brought the nearest bag out into the light. Inside it were pieces of scrap metal—nails, a rusted bike chain, dented food tins, coils of copper wire, a few short lengths of pipe. Small items, easy to carry. Scattered amongst the scrap were two or three handfuls of coins. I replaced the bag and slid the cinder block back into place.

As I returned to the stairwell entrance, it occurred to me how strange it was that when I'd given the drifter money he'd taken only the coins, leaving the note to be carried away by the wind. And I thought how strange it was that he had been limping, a little less each day, as I'd watched him those mornings from my corner seat in the café. I hadn't caught sight of the right side of his face but I bet myself, as I entered the apartment building and ascended the stairs, that it would still be bruised and swollen from the previous week's injuries.

I called Ashton.

'Just a sec, I need to find a quiet spot. There are kids everywhere.'

'You ever get a feeling like you're headed for inevitable disaster?'

'Yeah. Every time I reach for the biscuit tin.'

'Those biscuits are meant to be eaten.'

'You feeling all right, my friend?'

'I'm just stuck in a rut, really. I feel as though nothing's ever going to change in life. Like, imagine that every decision we make spawns a new version of the world and a new version of ourselves.'

'As in the quantum multiverse?'

'Sure. But what if all those versions of myself, if I could observe them, what if I found out they all end up badly? I sometimes wonder if I'm simply incapable of serving my own best interests.'

'That's pretty heavy, my friend. And cryptic. Any more details you'd care to share?'

'It's unfair to be laying this on you. I'm just this weird customer, right?'

'No. You're my friend.'

'Friendship complicates matters.'

'They say there's a storm coming. Stargazing will be cancelled tonight. I'll be knocking off early, if you want to relax a bit, talk, you know? It gets pretty wild up here on the hill during a storm.'

'Maybe tomorrow,' I said.

I let Ashton's return calls go straight to voicemail. There wasn't a single thing he could do to help.

*
**

He was late the next morning, that version of myself who wandered the streets, whose body, like mine, was not entangled in the cyclical resetting of time, and whose blood no doubt also ran thick with technology from the distant future.

When he eventually shuffled past, I left the café and trailed him, maintaining a sly distance. He spent the day as expected: scouring the streets for metallic objects, asking strangers for change and filling his pockets with everything that he gathered. Late afternoon, he returned to the apartment car park to secure his bounty behind the cinder block.

Near the top of the driveway, as he was returning from the skip, I stepped out of the shadow of the building and into his path. I held out a palmful of shining coins. He moved towards me with his cupped hands raised. The right side of his face was a wash of purple and yellow, like a dawn sky.

'Hello,' I said. 'Do you remember who I am?'

He stood, listening carefully.

'Chrononaut,' he said.

'Yes,' I said, and moved closer to him. I tipped the coins into the cup of his hands, and our flesh briefly touched. He panicked at the sensation and fled. The coins scattered across the asphalt, flashing like sparks in the late sun.

I ran after him but pulled up short when he reached the roadside. Without a glance in either direction, he darted across the road and three vehicles came within a centimetre of clearing him off his feet.

*
**

I wasn't the type of agent experienced in shadowing individuals, my objectives being focused on macro social and political observations. But with a target as oblivious as the drifter, it was easy. And something in the routine of tailing him invigorated me—the thrill of voyeurism, I suppose—until it became just that, another routine. He took buses all across the city. I didn't pursue him down every street, but I mapped the routes he took. He cycled through them habitually. It was yet another predictable pattern. The only notable change was in the volume of metal objects he amassed by the time I gave up the tailing game, he'd filled his fifth shopping bag.

*
**

The looping was unquestionably and vastly frustrating, but to my exhausted mind it also began to seem like an opportunity. Couldn't the rules that defined the looping also allow me to unburden myself, given the daily reset of time, and therefore the daily reset of the lives and minds of the people around me?

I attempted, one morning, to share a secret with the barista.

'Today's the sixth, right?' I asked.

'All day long,' the barista said, staring at my beard. 'Christmas is just around the corner, eh.'

'Christmas is a strange time of year.'

'So what'll it be?'

'Long black,' I said. Then, 'Eventually Christmas will become an unsayable word—censored outright. You won't be around for this, don't worry. In fact, you won't even remember what I'm about to tell you by the time tomorrow rolls around.'

'Ah-huh?'

'In about two hundred years, the Christmas Revolution, as it will be called at first—and which is essentially a global protest against widespread food shortages, due to prejudiced distribution rather than availability of resources—creates a major crossroads for the controlling states—'

'I'd believe that.'

'—throughout the global republic, culminating in armed in-fighting amongst ostensible allies. Nobody comes off well from this military sparring and the republic is left in bloody tatters.'

'War's always the answer with governments, eh?' the barista said, an uptick of uncertainty creeping into his voice.

'Christmas is ultimately bowdlerised, and the occasion is replaced over the following century by increasingly nationalistic ceremonies, each of them particular to the individual countries of the former republic, in terms of their festive practices, but general to all countries in the basic goal of instilling protectionist impulses in every member of every living generation—'

The barista scoffed. He looked down the short length of the queue behind me and shrugged at the customers, mouthing, *One minute.*

'—right down to baby in the bassinet. *Ten Fingers, Ten Toes, a Full Clip of Ammo!* is an actual catchphrase used during one specific but basically representative festive season, in this one specific but basically representative country.'

'Mate,' the barista whispered. 'That's a bit dystopian.'

'It is,' I agreed. 'And it's just one example. It's my job to travel back in time from the future, to observe and report on historical pressures that, even prior to the republic's formation, may have led—'

'That's three-fifty, ta,' the barista said, loud enough for everyone waiting behind me to hear.

I paid and took my usual place in the corner.

The barista and several of the customers glanced towards me every so often, as though I might at any moment upend a table, or worse.

'Long black? Excuse me, long black? This you?' the waitress timidly asked.

I accepted my coffee then promptly retreated to my apartment, leaving a wake of relieved sighs behind me.

I felt no relief, having simply humiliated myself. There was one other person who might understand my situation, but accessing the drifter's thoughts seemed like drawing water from a dry well.

I waited for the middle of the day, a window of time when he was typically traversing Wellington, then shined a flashlight into the earthen cavity behind the cinderblock.

Seven bags.

What drove him? It was clear that he kept up his routine not because he was condemned to, like everyone else in the world, but because he wanted to.

I wondered if he understood his actions or if his routine was mechanical. Was there anything truly alive inside his skull? Did his actions have real purpose, or was he only obeying some corrupted instruction encoded in the fritzed circuitry of his brain? Did he possess any memories, or any ideas about the future and the past? Did he conceive of himself as a whole person? And if he was a wasted version of myself, what kind of dreadful personal decay curve could I expect to endure?

In a way, the inevitability of my—his, our—suffering meant there was nothing to lose in the meantime. Didn't it?

*
**

Although I was unwilling to risk embarrassing myself in front of Ashton with the kind of confession I'd made in the café, I maintained the habit of calling him daily, in the hope that hearing his voice would help pull me back from madness, or at least from committing acts of madness.

I was desperate to understand what was happening, to find a solution to the looping. Each evening I fell into unconsciousness at 23:46, the moment of the reset, and awoke sometime later with a terrible anxiety sucking at my guts and mind. The feeling was worse than the deep apprehension I'd felt—as every time-traveller feels—when first surrendering to the vast slipstreams of the multiverse. The feeling was one of claustrophobia, of being trapped in a narrow and lightless tunnel extending forever in both directions and from which the best chance of escape was to scratch through the hard rock of the very mountain that enclosed me.

'Just a sec,' Ashton said on the other end of the phone. 'I need to find a quiet spot. There are kids everywhere.'

'It'd be cool to catch up tonight, if the offer's still there,' I said, remembering too late that Ashton had not yet made such an offer, not in this iteration of today. In his bubble of time, we hadn't talked in over a fortnight.

'Um, sure?' Ashton said. 'Remind me?'

'Relax a bit, talk, you know,' I said. 'They say there's a storm coming. I guess stargazing will be cancelled?'

I was sitting on my bed, keeping a close eye through the bedroom doorway on Vincent, who I'd tied to a chair in the kitchen. I'd improvised a gag using a damp washcloth and packing tape. I'd also emptied a bookshelf and dragged it across the front door, and shut up all the curtains and windows.

I had named the drifter 'Vincent', although he and I likely shared the same name—just as we shared the same genetics and the same technology in our blood. Only, he seemed unable to confirm his name for me. Nonetheless, assigning him a name that was different from my own made everything that little bit easier.

Not easy, but easier.

I should be forthright about this. I had abducted Vincent with the intention of hurting him, perhaps even killing him. If it came down to that.

'You're right about the storm,' Ashton said. 'I'll be knocking off early.'

'Great. You can help me bury the body.'

'Always happy to lend a hand, my friend.'

'Or maybe we ought to use a bathtub of lime.'

'Although there's no way you're not joking, the way you said that was not very funny.'

'Right. No blood on my hands.'

'Something else on your mind?'

'Have you ever looked at yourself in a mirror and thought, I recognise this person but I have no idea who they truly are?'

'You definitely need to relax a bit, my friend.'

'Without a doubt. See you later?'

'Sure. I have to get back to work,' Ashton said. 'The next planetarium show's in five minutes: "Nature—the Original World Wide Web". How's my voice?'

'A little agitated,' I said. 'Tone it down for the kids.'

I dropped the phone onto the bed, picked up the long-bladed carving knife and went through the living room into the kitchen. Vincent's fingers were fumbling at the ropes. I'd taken a few pointers from a crime drama that I'd watched over and over and over again on television.

'What do you know?' I said. 'Tell me.'

I caught a pucker in the tape with the knife and sliced through. The flap of tape doubled back on itself. Vincent let the washcloth fall from his mouth and onto his lap, then the floor.

I took the seat opposite him.

'What kind of version of me are you?'

Vincent stared.

'Let's talk timelines. Were you spawned from my world, and did things then turn personally to shit in your parallel world?'

He said nothing.

'Or are you a version of me from the near future of this world, a near future in which things get worse for me?'

He stared and stared.

It was sad to watch his unresponsive expression, the sense of an almost complete emptiness inside him. I felt that Vincent owed me an answer, a denial or a confirmation of our basic relationship, or what he understood of it. I imagined a black box inside his skull. Inside the box was the key to my future, but Vincent couldn't access it. He was the keeper of the black box and nothing more. It was a frightful thought, that he might represent both some truth about myself and the denial of that truth.

I stood and flashed him the knife, close so that he could see the gleam of the bade. Then I pressed the tip to his cheek, not quite firmly enough to pierce the skin.

I sat back down.

'How did you end up in this continuity? What's the last thing you remember before arriving here?'

'Chrononaut,' he said.

'Yes,' I said. 'I am, as are you.'

'Spaceman.'

I stood and slapped him with the back of my hand. He whimpered and I showed him the knife again.

'Your limited vocabulary is unhelpful.'

He said nothing.

'If I stuck this knife between your ribs and into your heart, would you die in this world or would you die in your own? Would another version of you show up like some factory replacement?'

'Shadow,' he said.

'If I did stab you through the heart, would I die too?'

I turned the knife around, pointed its tip against my chest and held it there. Vincent stared and I stared back and we sat there like that, neither of us saying anything.

I wondered about his life—the simplest parts of it and how different from mine they might be. I wondered whether his parents were still alive. I wondered what his childhood home had looked like. I wondered who he'd loved, what punishments he'd received, what his pleasures were, what the worst thing was that he'd done to another human being. What he thought of me.

'You're an arsehole,' I said. 'But I'm an arsehole too.'

He said nothing.

'I may as well go first,' I said, after a long moment.

I held out one arm in front of me, the sleeve rolled up past the elbow. It was only fair to begin the experiment with myself. I sucked in a breath, raised the carving knife up high, then hacked the blade down into my forearm. The blade was narrow and might not strike bone, but it would leave an unmistakable wound, an unmistakable scar.

Blood welled rapidly and began to spill across the linoleum floor. I dropped the knife and groped around for the towel that I'd placed nearby. I was dimly aware of Vincent yelping and banging the chair up and down as he battled against his restraints.

I located the towel and wrapped it around my arm. Using my free hand and my mouth, I attempted a knot, but the towel's bulk and the pain in my shaking, injured arm made it difficult. I settled for winding the packing tape crudely around the towel to fix it in place, and I tore the tape with my teeth, the bitter taste of adhesive strong on my tongue. All the while Vincent kept up his animal noises and his banging.

I collected the knife, then stood and moved behind him.

'Don't worry,' I said, grimacing. 'Things will be all right.'

I crouched down and slipped the knife through the ropes around his ankles and wrists, severing the bonds with graceless sawing motions. Vincent hurried to the door and dragged the bookshelf aside, then scurried out into the corridor, packing tape still stuck to his face. I listened as his lumbering footsteps fell along the corridor and faded as he reached the stairwell and began his descent.

I set to painfully stitching up my wound.

I did not see Ashton later. I sent him a text pleading exhaustion and stayed at home, cleaning up the kitchen then watching the lightning storm from my armchair until I dropped once more into unconsciousness.

*
**

I took several days to recuperate before acting again, though I kept an eye on Vincent's movements. He maintained his habits and—surprisingly, given our bloody encounter—I could always spy him by the skip in the late afternoon.

He quickly learned to expect me. After I'd recovered enough, my good arm managed the tough work of tackling him, while the hand of my bad arm clamped the soaked rag over his mouth and nose.

He was a reasonable fighter, and I had no luck most days.

Once I had successfully secured him in my apartment again, I eagerly checked his forearm, but discovered no sign of a wound. I did notice, however, a fresh-looking scar on his cheek—from the incident with the Commodore outside the café—which had revealed itself from beneath the bruising. I searched my own cheek and determined that I did not possess the same scar. Here was proof, then, that Vincent was not of my immediate future, and I was not of his. Without doubt, we were parallels of each other—but the precise nature of our relatedness was still a mystery.

What that meant in terms of his specific knowledge of our situation, I could not guess. I could only say that maintaining a proximity to the apartment—and perhaps to me—remained important to him in his work of collecting bags upon bags of metallic miscellany, despite the threat to his wellbeing that I posed. During our interviews, I never managed to extract more than the same three words from him.

Spaceman. Chrononaut. Shadow.

Yet, I soon began to wonder whether a hot network of neurons inside his brain might light up at the recognition of a significant formula, like headlights picking out shapes in the fog.

I again roped him down while he was still unconscious. As I waited for him to come out of his fumy daze, I barricaded the front door. When he revived, I read aloud from a selection of my notebooks.

'Speak up—or nod or tap a foot—if you recognise anything unusual, any errors, anything at all,' I told him.

I read him page after page after page.

He stared so intently his eyeballs began to dry out. I had to remind him to blink. We eventually took a break and I flicked his face with ice water from a bowl, to keep him alert. As I returned the bowl to the bench, he charged, still strapped to the chair, and drove me hard against the kitchen wall, knocking me out cold. When I came round, he was gone.

So was my kitchen cutlery.

*
**

I number and sort all of my notebooks, firstly by thematic investigation and then chronologically. It's a system with obvious virtues in aiding quick lookups, but it's useful in other scenarios. For example—in restoring the notebooks to the correct order, after their having been placed aside while the bookshelf is repurposed as a barricade. It was in this way that I noticed the notebook between 02.11 and 02.13 had gone missing.

The question of its location was cleared up by a search of the earthen cavity behind the loose cinder block in the car park. It was surprising that Vincent had been capable of spotting a notation of significant interest after all, and even more surprising was what that notation pertained to. There was a single page in 02.12 that he'd dog-eared and bordered with obsessive loops of blue crayon.

The 'shadow space', as we'd dubbed it within my small circle of friends at the academy, was an idea we had speculated over in a fervour following a lecture on the mechanics of slipstreams—those electrifying passageways between compatible worlds of the multiverse.

'Divergence from the prime context—that is, from the clearest line of continuity connecting your start and end points,' the lecturer had said, 'represents the greatest threat to the success of any achronological journey. You do not want to find yourself in a universe in which tyrannical arthropods rule the earth. The second greatest threat is the actuation of an overlap between continuities—a shadowy intersection where two universes collide.'

Two universes colliding! That could only mean the mutual destruction of both universes, our young minds reasoned. We saw the intersection as an enormous field of dark churning energy flowing between the condemned universes, accelerating their expansion, tearing them apart at the seams.

It never occurred to us that the intersection might be a thin slice of common space, a portion of one world overlaying a portion exactly like it on a second world, their two realities mapped together. That the intersection might be bound in time as well as in space—by the span of a single day, for example. And that another human being, perhaps one just like ourselves, might be implicated in this cosmic clusterfuck, sucked through from one reality to the other. A shadow caught in a world of shadows.

*
**

I departed from routine that night and shunned the comfort of my armchair. Instead, I lay on the asphalt, in the middle of the car park. The storm crashed above me. Grimy floodwater pooled and eddied around me, running over my limbs, tugging at my shirt, filling my shoes. The unchanged, perfectly regular signatures on the time machine's core played as a double image across my vision. Again, at the dead hour of 23:46, I slipped into that baneful and familiar blackness, where I dreamed of snakes whose skins were decorated in the patterns of the cosmos, whose underbellies pulsed with flashes of electric blue as they uncoiled from the sky and slithered down to swallow pieces of the earth and suck at the oceans until the world was wholly devoured.

I woke with their hissing still in my ears. I was dry through and through. The pre-dawn sky was free of any clouds and the stars gleamed like granules of shattered glass under streetlights.

A darkness spread across the firmament. There above me was Vincent's face. He was staring down at me, laughing through his teeth.

He had vanished between the cars, out to the street, lost to the night, by the time I scrambled to my feet.

Later that morning, as I waited for my coffee, I thought about the way Vincent had held himself, looming over me, his arms across his chest like he was cradling a baby. I thought about his laughter. I thought about my routine check of the time machine's signatures, which I'd undertaken before lying down amongst the cars, unsure which world I occupied on that patch of asphalt and from which world the rain fell as it cascaded around me.

I dashed past the woman in the white T-shirt and overalls, careful to avoid her elbows, and out onto the street. Behind me a voice called, 'Long black? Excuse me, long black? This you?'

The over-sink cupboard in my kitchen was empty. The time machine was nowhere to be found. Ditto my spare house key. Vincent's bags of scrap metal were missing from the cinder block cavity.

I stood outside for perhaps an hour, in the recessed doorway to the internal stairwell, waiting for Vincent to come winding through the car park, perhaps lugging the time machine under one arm, or still cradling it, or slinging it around in one of his plastic shopping bags, while the thought grew in my mind that it was not his intention to come back at all.

I phoned Ashton but his lunch break had ended. I left him a voicemail telling him I'd appreciated his friendship and that he had no idea what his company had meant to me. I told him I hoped we'd see each other again—if not in this world then another one.

There were half a dozen bus routes that Vincent preferred in his journeys across Wellington. I ticked them off one by one. I stared shamelessly into the faces of the people in their seats and in the aisles, drawing scornful mutters and sharp looks in return. As the streets moved past the windows of the bus, I inspected the usual paths that Vincent took. I disembarked and asked pedestrians if they'd seen my brother—a twin, no beard. At the final stop in the journey out to Island Bay, as the day turned dark and the rain set in, I saw his eyes peering through the glass of the window. He jumped when I jumped, then I noticed the length of his whiskers—they were as long as my own, not the coarse stubble that Vincent managed to maintain. My reflection receded as I slumped back into my seat.

The street gutters were flooding as I boarded the last bus on my list, the scenic route from downtown to Miramar Heights, following the weaving coastline from Oriental Parade. The first bolt of lightning flared across the sky as the bus pulled into a stop near a colossal wind wand that rose starkly from the grass beside a small marina. The sculpture's elongated needle pivoted severely downwards, threatening to pierce the roofs of vehicles as they passed by. The needle was supported in a gimbal atop a tall, broad-based concrete cone, around the side of which—as another fork of lightning flashed violently and the bus merged into the thinning traffic—I caught sight of a gaunt man carrying several shopping bags.

I called out to the driver to pull over, and at the next stop, a hundred metres down the road, I stepped out into the heavy rain. 'Push the damn button next time, if you want to get off,' the driver barked, before the folding doors of the bus snapped shut.

Vincent was turned away from me, emptying out the last of his bags, when I arrived. Littered across the grass and glinting in the rain and volatile light were hundreds of small metallic objects, building into a pile around the wind wand's base.

'Chrononaut! Spaceman!' I shouted. He turned to face me and a gust snatched the last of the empty bags from his hand, sending it high into the air above the road. 'The machine you took from my kitchen—I can help you with it,' I said. Vincent bared his teeth the same as when he'd stood over me in the car park laughing, and then he returned to his work. He picked up a length of cable made from woven copper wire. One end was attached to the gimbal that held the needle. Vincent tracked the rest of the cable around to the other side of the base.

'Hey!' A man's voice broke through the noise of the wind and the rain. 'Is that you, my friend?' Ashton was striding towards me. His car was parked halfway up the kerb, hazard lights flashing, just beyond the reach of the needle bending low in the buffeting wind. The drawstring hood of his raincoat was tight around his face. In the growing dark, he looked like a paper silhouette, the crinkled edges already giving way to the tearing force of the wind.

I raised a hand in tentative greeting.

'I hope you don't mind,' he said as he came near. 'I looked up your address on the observatory's database after I got your voicemail. You really scared me, man. I swung by your apartment to check you hadn't done anything crazy. I was just pulling up when I saw you hop on a bus.' He grabbed me by my shoulder and looked into my face. 'Well, I was pretty sure it was you. That beard looks legit. Did you take a serum? It's got some real length.' He stood back again, wiped the rain from his face and then looked at the objects strewn across the grass. 'I lost you in all the traffic, but here we are. What's all this stuff, and are you all right? I mean—whoa!' Ashton snapped his head around to look at Vincent, who'd reappeared. He turned back to me. 'Okay. I didn't realise,' he said. 'I'm Ashton. I'm a friend—of your brother's?'

'No, it's me,' I said. 'This is kind of awkward.'

Ashton stood with his lips parted, raindrops slipping between them.

I struggled against the urge to tell him what was happening. I had frightened him badly and he had responded with the urgency and care of a genuine friend. Didn't he deserve some honesty? I checked behind me. Vincent was crouched down, piling up a section of objects that had slipped away from the base.

'Hey?' Ashton said, touching my arm below the bandage where I'd experimentally attacked my own flesh.

I turned back. Ashton wiped his face again. I could explain later that the man behind me was not my twin but a shadow version of me whom I had dragged here from some other existence. Later, if it ever arrived, I could explain the beard and the bandage.

'Don't worry. Things will be all right,' I said, and recalled the moment in my kitchen when I'd said the same words to Vincent, both of us desperate and afraid, but only one of us holding a bloodied carving knife in his hand. 'Give me a few minutes, okay? But could you please wait in the car?'

Ashton nodded slowly, several times, as if it might trigger a greater level of understanding.

He began moving away. After a few steps he turned and cupped his hands to his mouth. 'I'm having trouble digesting all of this,' he shouted. 'Hurry up, yeah?' I gave him a thumbs-up and he continued towards the flashing lights.

Vincent appeared, at first glance, to be watching Ashton. But his eyeline was higher—his eyes were on the tilting needle. He was counting off on one hand in sets of five. In his other hand I saw he held a metal pipe, angled at one end to create a pike.

'Put the weapon down—please!' I yelled. I tried to work out how to tackle Vincent without receiving the sharpened metal shaft in my abdomen.

A break came in the wind. Vincent drove the pike into the ground, his eyes fixed on the needle as it whipped towards the pulsing sky. A white light spilled over us. Vincent opened his mouth wide—whooping with pleasure or pain. Then threads of fire tore through my body, and the world was turned off.

'When I got to the car, I grabbed the tyre iron from the boot, in case something bad was going down,' Ashton said, his voice low. 'I was walking back to you guys when it happened. The rain looked like static on TV, in the strobe lightning. Then your bodies warped across the space between you. It was extremely weird, when you had these two heads that were melding into one head.'

It was, at last, Thursday.

We'd barely slept.

The woman in front of us in the queue was wearing a dark purple pantsuit. She ordered a triple-shot cappuccino, swiped her card and punched in her PIN. I cast my eyes towards the table of complimentary newspapers then around the room. The woman in the white T-shirt and overalls was nowhere to be seen. The hum of conversation that filled the café contained rhythms and harmonies that were entirely fresh to my ears.

'Mate, whaddaya after?' the barista said.

'Long black,' I said. 'Extra shot.'

I rolled double sixes and received my coffee gratis.

'Lucky, future boy,' Ashton said.

'Quit it,' I said.

Back in the privacy of my apartment, Ashton sipped his coffee and browsed my shelves of notebooks.

'I truly believed you were a freelance researcher. Sociology, anthropology, something like that.'

'I am. Or I was, maybe.'

'You really feel okay?' Ashton took a seat beside me on the couch. 'I mean, think of the state of that wind wand. Split down the middle—totally splintered! I could actually see a zigzag burned into it, tracing the path the lightning took.'

He looked down at my arm, the bandage now gone and the tender pink scar showing, but said nothing more.

'It hurt a lot,' I said. 'Though the lightning didn't exactly touch me.'

My blood had lit up when the lightning struck and even as Ashton and I sat in my apartment several hours later, I could feel a strange heat, a fluid radiance, in my limbs, like slow lightning was moving through me.

'You know, I'm pretty handy with machines. You ever hear of RoboWars? I was the reigning national champ, three years running.' Ashton gestured towards the time machine's casing on the coffee table. 'Looks like a coffee thermos, really. A capacity, I'd say, of about twelve cups.'

The signatures on the time machine's exposed core were all flat lines, meaning it may as well have been a regular thermos. Although, the steadily glowing tether light indicated that it was at some level still operational, and still connected to the chronochips in my bloodstream.

I ran a hand over my beard. It was thick and bushy. I had decided to keep it until my next step was clear. I'd need a job, something to cover the rent at least, before my supply of counterfeit digidollars finally ran out.

I wondered about going into teaching, maybe history.

'Anyway, we can tinker with it,' Ashton said. 'We'll get you back safely to wherever and whenever you belong.' He laughed. 'It's mad! You must have some incredible stories to tell.'

'The present is incredible enough.'

He reached across the couch and lightly traced the scar on my arm, then slipped his fingers beneath mine and squeezed my hand. I offered nothing in response at first, then ran my thumb over his knuckles, feeling their smooth topography of ridges and valleys.

I thought of the absurd canvas banner back at mission control. GOOD LUCK on one side, WELCOME HOME on the other. Maybe my luck was good as things were. This present wasn't perfect, but it was better than the future. Of course, things were due to turn a long corner. But for now, what would it matter if I stayed on awhile? The mountain had been cracked open, with Ashton's help, and there was a feeling of light on my skin, the feeling of human warmth.

'No rush,' I said. 'They'll hardly notice that I'm gone.'

The Difficult Art of Bargaining

Are we to introduce ourselves to our new neighbours as a pair of beggars? Worse—introduce ourselves as beggars to a friend of our dear son?

It seems we are.

My husband says, 'Look. A specialty butcher, right around the corner. No need to forsake a nice cut of meat.'

'A stew of shin steak,' I say to my husband, 'is the best we can expect.'

My husband says, 'Liv, darling,' and hunches over the steering wheel. He has a high tolerance for failure, my husband, but a rather low tolerance for criticism.

'Our pension will be stretched thin as filo just to cover the rent,' I say. 'Have you forgotten we are starting over with nothing? Worse—starting over with less than nothing?'

'Liv, darling,' my husband says. 'We must face the future bravely. We must do what we can to get on. We mustn't overburden our David and his Molly.'

My husband is not incorrect.

I say to my husband, 'We are a burden unto ourselves.'

I touch my headscarf, feeling the delicate silk between my fingers. Its colours had spoken to me from a dark corner of the wardrobe, where it must have lain for about ten years. It was like retrieving a forgotten memory, as in those moments before sleep when the mind coughs up its more peculiar suggestions. I discovered it the day before we departed, the day before a new, young family was due to start filling those emptied rooms and hallways with the routines and memories, wonderful and dreadful and all things in-between, of their own lives. I finger the hem of the scarf, feeling the breeze tug at it through the open window, feeling wisps of hair flit against the blade of my hand, across my temple and my ear, as we near the location of the rental apartment that we shall soon occupy.

'We have not lost everything,' my husband says, straightening his spine against the driver's seat. 'We have twelve boxes full of photo albums, chinaware, clothing, a hundred trinkets. We have our big bed. We have our memories. We have good, healthy souls.'

'How much is a soul worth?'

At the unripe age of thirteen, I watched my mother wither away from lung cancer, and inherited the daily care of four siblings and a heartbroken father. Then as now, the feeling was not one of spiritual solace but of cold nakedness. If there's a supreme being in the sky, he might consider getting off his supreme backside and lending a hand. No, I don't believe in souls. I believe in the vicissitudes of luck and, more so, I believe in human folly. My husband is a hopeful man, to a fault. He believes all manner of nonsense.

'Could you fetch for the price of your good, healthy soul, a brand-new sofa?' I ask my husband. 'With large, plush cushions?'

'The sofa looked very comfortable, in the photographs.'

'We shall see. A picture can tell a thousand lies.'

We approach the driveway to the apartment building from a direction different from that which the rental agent took, when she drove us here for our first viewing, and then our second, and our third. 'Third time's the charm,' she cheerily said. 'This little box?' I replied. 'Hardly any charm at all.' We said yes, of course. What else could we do?

'Here we are then,' my husband says.

The parking is outdoors, at the rear of the apartment building. This rust bucket won't survive a year, exposed to Wellington's malicious climate. We will be forced to trade down once again, if such a reduction is possible. 'It'll cost you in the long run,' our son said of this car, and in the middle of the yard, under the sharp eye of the fat little salesman, he gave the bonnet a rattling slap. 'I'm happy to keep driving you around, until you're back on your feet.' Our son and his girlfriend, Molly, had done so much already, providing us with shelter and helping to ease our debts. 'David,' my husband said, with a nod to the salesman, 'thank you, but we need our independence.' My husband then gripped our son's shoulder to convey, wordlessly so as not to be argued against, that our regaining independence would mean the same for him and Molly.

In the mirror of the sun visor I fix my headscarf, which has become loose in the wind, along with several loops of hair. I unknot the scarf, letting it drop across my shoulders, then draw my hair back and secure it again with one of Molly's black hair-ties. The scarf's swirling colours against the subtle cream of my dress seems a pleasingly bold touch. I knot the scarf lightly around my throat and fluff the tips, then tuck the sun visor back into place and step out of the car.

We walk around to the front of the grounds, where my husband stops to stare up at the building—admiringly, if his smile is to be believed. The façade of the main entrance might be charming, recalling my days on the amateur stage, if it weren't so tarnished. Two stonework pillars are topped by an arch, in the centre of which the twin masks of Tragedy and Comedy stare out with their frozen expressions. I don't recall having either cried or laughed in months. The façade is original, so the rental agent informed us—from the early part of last century, when the building was a repertory theatre. 'All the world's a stage,' she said, and I wished a trapdoor would open up beneath her. Above the arch, the name REPERTORY APARTMENTS is painted in peeling black letters. The building proper is concrete, mean-looking. Faded blue with faded orange trim around the windows, complementing the dribbling rust stains on the downpipes. Rust has become the colour of our lives. Our rented apartment is located on the bottom floor. Our son's friend with the sofa is on the top floor.

'We owned a quarter acre,' I say to my husband. 'Now we have this.'

'Liv,' my husband says. 'Darling.'

Inside the entrance, to the left, is the elevator. A pale-blue door, paint chipped, conceals a brass scissor gate that my husband, with difficulty, drags open. We enter and he closes the gate with a vicious snap, then presses the button for level four.

'Hold steady,' my husband says, then as the elevator begins to rise, in a sing song voice, 'He-e-e-re we go-o-o!'

The concrete floors, defaced by haphazard markings of pencil and permanent marker, slide by on the other side of the gate. The elevator shudders to a stop and my husband releases me into the top-floor corridor with a pat on my bottom.

'Ladies first.'

The mauve carpet has been faded by years of sunlight falling through the street-side windows and dirtied by ingrained layers of ever-gathering dust. Our son's friend's apartment is at the farthest end.

My husband knocks on the door with three firm raps.

A young man, perhaps in his mid-thirties, opens the door.

'Hello! David's parents? I'm Ashton.'

'Pleased to meet you,' my husband says, squeezing the young man's slender hand. 'George—and this is my wife, Liv.'

I nod politely.

'We'll be neighbours in a week or so,' my husband says.

'David said,' the young man says. 'Welcome to the block. Come in, please, just to your right.'

'We used to live on a quarter acre,' I say. 'We've never lived in the city before.'

'Oh, yes,' the young man says. 'It's funny the way things turn out, eh?'

'Funny?' I stand in the corridor as my husband, blocking the doorway, gazes at pictures on the hallway wall—reproductions of Dali's flabbily draped clocks and a Monet of a lilac and grey cathedral.

'I mean,' the young man says, 'life can be very unfortunate. You'll find that the building is well located. Right on a good bus route, and easy to get into town and to the hospital, and whatnot.'

'My husband bankrupted us,' I say.

'Liv,' my husband says. 'Darling.'

'It sounds like you've had a rough time. David mentioned you were basically robbed by the, ah, the'—the young man pokes a finger in the air—'Hot Chips? Big Chips?'

'Big Chips Investments,' my husband says, taking my hand. We shuffle down the apartment's short hallway. My husband says, 'Never again.'

The young man's apartment is larger than ours. I suppose they must typically be more spacious, the apartments on the top floors, the penthouses, although there is no great sense of luxury about this place—it isn't that manner of apartment building. Nevertheless, my husband and I are certainly on the bottom rung, where I suspect we shall remain without the opportunity to regain even moderate luxuries for ourselves. A living room that can accommodate a complete sofa suite, for example, or a pleasant hobby room such as that into which the young man is leading us.

In the room, a desk sits beneath a window overlooking a narrow, overgrown alleyway. Beside the desk is a bookshelf filled with notebooks, and opposite the desk is the sofa. It's not as long or as deep or as plush as either of the sofas we were forced to sell for next to nothing. No doubt our new living room would accommodate it—but not generously. We would have to rethink the option of ottomans.

'Bloody tragic,' the young man says. 'I read that the scheme—really dirty—that it hurt a lot of people. Young folk, and people like yourselves.'

'David has been extremely kind to us,' I say. 'Subsequent to the investment souring.'

The sofa's deep chocolate fabric has faded to a burnt caramel along one half of the seatback's top and down the adjoining arm.

'We are humbled,' my husband says, 'to have a son like David.'

'He's a great guy,' the young man says. 'You did a fine job.'

'Thank you very much,' I say. 'I think David appreciates everything we've done for him.'

'David mentioned you've moved in with your partner?' my husband says.

'Yeah. He's at work at the moment.'

'Pity we can't meet him,' I say, immediately concerned that I have placed too much emphasis on the pronoun. My husband looks at me in a critical manner that I feel he has not earned. I fear the silence is growing heavy and that it may be misinterpreted by this young man, this friend of our son.

'What does he do, your partner?' I ask. 'And yourself, what do you do?'

'I work part-time at the Carter Observatory, in the Botanic Garden. Dylan teaches history at one of the local high schools, and moonlights as a writer. This humble abode suits us for now, while we're saving.'

'Plans?' I ask.

'Sort of a private venture. Don't worry, we're not looking for investors!' The young man laughs as if he has made a good joke. He stops, noticing that my husband and I have not joined him.

My husband's face is attentive regardless.

'A writer,' my husband cries, forever easily impressed. 'Does he write about historical subjects as well as teach them?'

'He used to be pretty interested in historical non-fiction,' the young man says. 'Now he tends to write about more immediate times and topics. The ordinary stuff that history boils away, as he reckons. If only walls could talk, especially in a place like this, eh? Don't worry, it's mostly fiction.' The young man pauses and drops his head slightly, encouraging us, I suppose, to believe that our privacy is not under threat. 'At any rate . . . moving in together, we found ourselves with a few extra bits and pieces. There's the sofa, of course. But also kitchen appliances, cutlery and whatnot, if you have any need—'

'We are all set for cutlery.' I find myself wiping my hands down my dress, smoothing out creases that are not there. I reach for my headscarf and touch only hair, forgetting the scarf has been relocated lower down. No doubt a rather nosy person, this writer, whatever reassurances the young man offers. Thankfully, I should think that my husband and I present little of interest as subject matter. And to presume that we wouldn't possess our own cutlery! I search for the soft silk at my throat, and my fingertips meet nothing but the stiff collar of my dress, the flesh of my neck. I glance down, then around the room. The headscarf is nowhere to be seen. It has become lost—through my own damned carelessness. Where, where? Somewhere along the dusty corridor, in the grimy elevator, the crowded car park? The splash of colour in the sun-visor mirror is all I recall.

'Well, go on. Try it out,' the young man says, indicating the sofa.

I say to my husband—silently, with my eyes—you do it, you slump your body down onto that lumpy wreck. My husband comprehends the signal but is hesitant.

'Take a seat,' the young man urges. 'It's in good nick. Nice and firm, hasn't lost its spring.'

My husband reaches towards the faded sofa arm. His fingertips make contact first, then he presses his palm into the padding. He leans into it, bearing his weight down through his spread fingered hand.

'Five years old, David said you said?' I say, my fingers still feeling at my throat for the silk.

'Practically brand new,' the young man says.

My husband turns and lowers his backside, taking cautious aim, as if there is some chance he might miss the large and immobile target. Halfway down, he drops like a shot bull. The sofa bears him well, it should be said. My husband begins to bounce up and down, a grin spreading over his face. A cruel thought enters my mind—my husband has always been too willing to make a fool of himself.

'Oh,' he says. 'It is rather comfortable.'

My husband has difficulty getting back up he is so comfortable. The young man offers a hand but struggles to assist him. It seems that the young man will tumble down on top of my husband, but with a final heave the situation is avoided. Their faces are flushed when they stand shoulder to shoulder again.

'Yours for only fifty bucks,' the young man says.

I notice a dark stain on the seat cushion where my husband had seconds ago been resting his hand as he bounced like a big child. I choke on my breath, loudly like a hiccup.

'Fifty's a bargain,' the young man reiterates.

I look to my husband, hoping to signal futility—to signal that all used sofas are bound to be faded and filthy. In a word, unsavoury. I want to make it clear to my husband, that sucker for a bad deal, that of all the things that must be purchased over again, he will have to purchase a sofa new.

'We'll have a think,' I say.

'Tell you what,' the young man says. 'I won't consider any other offers for a couple of days. If you decide you do want it, I can help shift it downstairs—if Dylan or David are around to provide some extra muscle. Maybe on the weekend?'

My husband holds the elevator door open and I quickly exit into the corridor.

'A writer in our midst,' my husband says, stepping alongside me.

'Minding his own business, one hopes.'

'Best watch what you say, Liv, darling,' my husband says and, curse the man, he gives a little chortle. 'The walls have ears.'

A sudden series of quick, clomping footsteps outside heralds the arrival of a small boy, who flies in through the ground-floor entry, dashing past us and along the corridor, trailing a bright streak behind him.

'My scarf!'

My husband looks towards the boy, aged perhaps four or five.

'I'll hold him down while you nab the goods,' he says, nudging me with his elbow.

''Scuse me, sorry.' A woman stumbles past us, clutching several bags of groceries. She stops outside the apartment beside the one that will soon be ours and deposits her rustling bags on the ground. Their apartment must be no larger than our own—hardly big enough for a growing boy. Certainly a far cry from the family home that our David enjoyed as a child. Is there a park nearby, where the boy might burn off this overwhelming energy?

'Samuel—oi!' the woman calls out. 'Samuel, where did you find that?' The boy stops running and trudges over to the woman. 'Pass it here, please.' After a moment of consideration the boy holds out the scarf and she plucks it from his grasp.

'Mum,' the boy says, 'it's my rainbow!'

'Sorry, is this yours?' the woman asks, turning to face us.

'It is,' I say. 'Thank you.'

'Mum! My rainbow!' the boy says.

The woman walks towards us. Closer now, in the cold light of the corridor, the headscarf appears somehow

different, somehow changed. Was there always that twist of
charcoal amongst the livelier colours?

'We'll be neighbours in a week or so,' my husband says.
'Right next door, that'll be us.' He offers his hand and the
woman shakes it. 'I'm George,' my husband says. 'This is my
wife, Liv.'

'Sally,' says the woman.

'Mum!' says the boy.

'Sam,' the woman says, 'come and say hello to the new
people moving in.'

The boy joins his mother. He looks up at us and mutters a
small hello, then tugs at the scarf dangling from his mother's
grip.

'No, Sam. This belongs to Liv. Give it back to Liv, please.'

The boy raises his hands and she drapes the scarf across
his palms. His young fingers close around the flowing silk,
and the colours, even the charcoal, seem to shimmer. The
boy turns to me, the scarf raised, bright fabric spilling
through his fingers.

What is it to let one more thing go?

I say to the boy, 'Hold on to it, if you like, Sam. If you
keep this rainbow safe, it will bring you and your mother
good luck.'

'Mum,' the boy says. 'Good luck!'

The woman raises her eyebrows at me, and I nod.

'What do you say? Sam, what do you say to Liv?'

'Thank you,' the boy says, then takes off down the
corridor, the scarf twirling through the air.

My husband offers to help the woman with her groceries,
and after the job is completed she promises to invite us
around for dinner. 'In a fortnight or so?'

'In a fortnight or so,' my husband confirms.

In the car park, as my husband reverses the rust bucket, bringing its rear bumper terribly close to a skip that has been squeezed up against the climbers and the sagging bushes, I say, 'We could cover it with a throw.'

'Hm?' my husband says.

'The sofa. You must have noticed the fading on the seatback and arm, that blotch on the seat cushion. We could cover it with a throw. Perhaps the gold and purple one— with the embroidered elephants.'

'Or we could purchase a new throw,' my husband says. 'No need to forsake every last nice thing in the world. The sofa is, after all, a smidge below budget.'

'A new throw?'

'Yes, Liv, darling.' Then, twisting his hands back and forth around the steering wheel, his foot gently pumping the accelerator, the rust bucket's engine squealing as we sit stationary in the apartment car park, my husband grins and says, 'Vroom, vroom!'

Jobs for Dreamers

A-hunting we will go

Daniel is growing pungent. No matter. The essentials are taken care of each day. He will shower in lukewarm water later with Amy. Hot water impacts costs, as does residual power usage. Around the apartment all unused appliances are unplugged. His laptop hums quietly amidst the nearly exhaustive silence. Daniel pierces open another can-mouth. *Psshht.* He sips the yeasty beer. Aaahhh. Not so bad. Consider the cost: a dozen for a dozen dollars. Some comforts have been afforded.

Daniel surveys the digital hinterland. He sallies forth and sets his traps with due care. The core mechanism of each trap is the same. The configuration and baiting of each trap is tailored. Each category of prey determines the precise configuration and baiting of each trap.

Category: Trades
Keywords: Labourer, apprentice
Salary: 35,000+ per annum
Employment type: Full-time/Part-time/Casual
Location: Wellington
Notification frequency: Immediately

Category: Hospitality
Keywords: Kitchen, dishwashing
Salary: 35,000+ per annum

Employment type: Full-time/Part-time/Casual
Location: Wellington
Notification frequency: Immediately

Category: Administration
Keywords: Filing, mailroom, back office
Salary: 35,000+ per annum
Employment type: Full-time/Part-time/Casual
Location: Wellington
Notification frequency: Immediately

Daniel the hunter awaits disturbance of his inbox. The ping of a prized specimen wandering into a precisely configured trap.

At the movies

'Which movie do you want to see?'
  'There are only disaster movies and operas.'
  'Do you want to see an opera?'
  'I want to wait for a refreshed schedule.'
  'We will come back next week.'
  'We cannot afford to see movies anyhow.'
  'Life must nonetheless be enjoyed.'
  'Life must nonetheless be endured.'
  'We will come back next week.'

Brute force

Each specimen is somehow unsuitable. Too lean to satisfy Daniel's debts. Or else too bold, too brutish. Would not be worth the goring he foresees in wrestling them to the ground. This despite the impressively serrated knife with handle stamped SKILLSET clasped firmly in his hand.

One kick of a hind leg and the specimen would bolt free, leaving Daniel with mottled hoof-shaped bruising, a nasty cut, something badly broken, something essential severed. Fortunately—the café. Part-time work for Amy. Half a block away, no associated transportation costs. Even on her rostered mornings, beautiful Amy sleeps beautifully.

Psshht. Aaahhh.

Daniel the hunter tampers with the bait. Tinkers with the configurations.

Stinking

I am turning the hot water up. I must at least wash for the sake of the customers, says Amy. You should take advantage of some hot water yourself. The sheets cling to you. They will soon be the only thing that clings to you—meaning I shall not, says Amy. I will not cling to you. Wash with soap. No more beer, you are drunk too often. You are drunk all the time, says Amy. You are rotting away like a vegetable. I know that you are doing your best. Stop crying. Why are you crying? Daniel, Daniel. Have you been to see the recruiter?

Certain limitations and practicalities

The recruitment agent sets aside her pen. She inspects Daniel's arms doubtfully.

'I could dig a hole as big as you like,' asserts Daniel.

The agent responds, 'It's not only a matter of physical aptitude.'

'Physical aptitude must be very transferrable.'

'In various industries it is important. Your experience lies within industries that do not emphasise physical ability or strength. These might be industries for which you are more appropriately qualified?'

'Office work is not possible.'

'Your experience pertains,' the agent says, fanning her large and fantastically ring-knobbed fingers on the table, 'to certain kinds of office-based employment.'

'Low-level administration duties would be all right. As a gap-fill, to get by.'

'How do you like to spend your time?'

'Pleasantly.'

'Pleasantly?'

'Dreamily.'

'And digging holes sounds pleasant?'

'If one may be permitted in the digging of a hole to dream.'

'A professional hole is typically dug through teamwork. Therefore the digging of a professional hole requires interpersonal savvy and active communication. And not a small degree of focus and attention. To avoid severing cables or pipes or other buried infrastructure.'

'I could operate within those parameters.'

'Do you enjoy reading books, watching movies, playing sports, completing crosswords, making art, solving differential equations, dining out? In regards to my earlier question.'

'I like to engage in entertainments, in order that I may dream larger dreams.'

'At some point questions of utility and social good must be considered. Have you seen a counsellor?'

'They said to follow my dreams.'

'They might have assumed certain limitations and practicalities?'

'They might have said so if they did. Are you checking your watch?'

'I'm afraid we're out of time.'

Honeycomb

Returning to the recruitment tower's elevators, Daniel bumps a table. A glass of dusty water shatters on the terracotta tiles of the reception area. 'I'm very sorry,' he says. An elderly woman dressed in a beekeeping suit smiles behind her sealed veil. 'No bother,' she says. The receptionist appears with a stack of paper towels and a brush and pan. 'Are you looking for work?' Daniel asks the beekeeper. 'I'm very, very sorry,' he says to the receptionist. 'No bother,' the receptionist says, extracting a thin glass splinter from her finger. 'I'm not here for work,' the beekeeper says. 'I'm looking to hire. I've been a beekeeper all my life. It's all I know. There's nothing else that I feel I could do at this point.' 'Could you dig a hole?' Daniel says. 'Not with these old arms. And I've got arthritis in my hands. I'm only keeping bees in my state because there's no one else to do the job.' The receptionist delicately transports the pan full of sopping paper towels and broken glass to a back room. 'Are you looking for work?' the beekeeper asks. 'I'm looking for money. Some kind of work must be involved.' 'Do you mind swarms of bees?' 'Don't you blow smoke to make them drowsy?' 'It doesn't always go as planned.' 'Might I dream from time to time while on the job?' 'Yikes! Well, you'd be too clumsy anyway.' From a pocket of her suit the beekeeper removes a small package wrapped with a strip of newspaper. She peels away the paper, revealing a stub of glistening honeycomb. The beekeeper unzips the bottom of her veil and pops the honeycomb into her mouth. 'Helps with several ailments, including arthritis,' she says. Her teeth and tongue twist around the sticky, waxy honeycomb. 'Only, I haven't eaten enough yet.' She offers Daniel a second stub, likewise wrapped in a strip of newspaper—a column from the death notices. The topmost notice begins: RECLUSIVE BEEKEEPER DORIS MORTIMER, 85, FOUND DEAD AMONGST HER HIVES.

At last, his elevator arrives. He enters the mirror-lined metal box and waves farewell, chewing the honeycomb so generously bequeathed to him. As he descends, Daniel wonders, Is it for the love of money or honey that the beekeeper's spirit works unceasingly? How sweet must the fruits of labour be for even death to be defied in their attainment? With the ambrosial gift dissolved, a ball of wax rests in Daniel's mouth.

In the labyrinth

The permutations across categories and sub-categories are endless. None suggest any real possibilities. What had Daniel hoped to find—was there something he was owed? A good life, a bad life, a moderate life, no life at all. He has stumbled into a labyrinth that reconfigures itself with every step, is full of dead ends, laced with snares, teeming with monstrous things moving in the shadows. Daniel the hunter, turned scavenging animal, stumbles through narrow passageways, brickwork scraping his hide, analytic eyes upon him, chilled voices muttering. The bull-headed minotaur says, *This one, huh? Let's have a look. Might be something we can use him for. Hold on a minute. No, no, no—send him back. Well, he seemed okay till you put him next to the others.*

Neither awake nor asleep, Daniel stumbles onwards.

Dream jobs

'How about collecting rubbish,' Daniel cries, wonderstruck.

'Refuse management?' Amy says.

'A job for dreamers.'

'I once dreamed I was a rectangle, hoping to become a triangle. I woke up absolutely sure that was the case and who

could have said it wasn't? My body felt rigid and geometric
and I didn't move for hours.'

'What do you mean?'

'I mean you only have to believe in something hard
enough.'

'Being is doing, not only believing.'

'You're right, I suppose.'

'And in the doing, the attainment of something.'

'Show me the money, honey.'

'It's a good idea. Refuse management. I'll see about any
openings with the council in the morning.'

'If you believe in it enough, I know you can do it.'

Position subject to review

Your position is subject to review.

The subject of your position is under review.

The position of you, the subject, is under review.

The review is subject to a position.

Position the subject: your review.

Review the subject: your position.

Our position on the subject is you're under review.

Our position is subject to review.

Review our position? Position your subject!

The position of the subject is subject to the subject under
    review.

Review your position, subject!

Your subject is the position of our review.

Our subject is the review of your position.

Scones

Amy in bed. Amy in bed with scones. Daniel unplugs the
microwave, unplugs the stereo, turns down the thermostat.

Amy and Daniel in bed. Daniel rises, unplugs the television.
Amy and Daniel in bed, a plate of quartered scones between
them. Scones without butter. Two each of: cheese scones,
bacon-and-zucchini scones, date scones spiced with
cinnamon. A meal coup from the café. A meal-time trifecta:
entrée, dinner and dessert. Don't be discouraged, says Amy.
Our rent is covered, the bills are nearly paid. Daniel unplugs
a lamp. They nibble unbuttered scones. Our savings are nil,
says Daniel. Amy squints at a scone. She pinches it tenderly.
The lattice of crusted cheese cracks. The scone's unbuttered
body crumbles. I'm afraid the scones are old, says Amy.
The old scones fill Daniel's belly almost wonderfully. He
licks crumbs from his fingers, crumbs from her fingers. He
leans to kiss Amy, upsetting the plate. Quartered scones
spill across the bedcovers. I zapped them briefly in the
microwave. I hoped they'd seem fresh, says Amy. I could eat
scones forever, says Daniel. We have been, or we will be, if
we're lucky, says Amy, as together they gather the scattered
scones in the moonlight.

Journey to the Edge

Reece scoops his forelock to the left then the right, hands held like claws. He lets it drop to the centre, the gelled triangle of hair reaching the bridge of his nose. He must know that it's perfect, but he checks it anyway in the long mirror—which interrupts the bare wall like a kind of passageway, one that only leads back to where you came from, taking you nowhere except to greet yourself. Reece sways on his feet and stares at his reflection, adjusting a strand of imaginary hair, slicking it back into line.

'Geometric as fuck,' he says.

'Where is it we're going?' I say.

'To the edge.'

'Where's that?'

'We'll go right to the edge, and maybe over.'

'Sounds dangerous.' I suck on my cigarette then blow smoke towards the open window beside the bed. A Kola can rests between my thighs, its metal skin sticking slightly to the pleather, and I tap ash into its mouth. 'So, what's the actual plan?'

He crouches and peers under the dresser. 'We're going to the edge, like I said, then I'm taking you home, then I'm going to Matt's, where I'll crash for the night, and then, tomorrow, he'll take me to the airport.'

'Right,' I say, giving up. 'How's Mutt keeping?'

'Charming as ever,' he says, standing up, casting around.

I have been friends with Reece longer, by several years, than Mutt has. We tried hanging out together, but quickly learned from that error. Reece now keeps us partitioned— and while he dislikes me using the name Mutt, the label fits. Mutt once stole eighty dollars from Reece, then blamed his own sister's boyfriend. Broke them up. But Mutt was grinning around smoothly rolled joints of quality grass for a month afterwards. At least he shared some with Reece and his sister, like a good mate, a good sibling. I learned all this when I later dated Mutt's sister, a disastrous stint that lasted about a week. She is as bad as her brother.

'Brisbane,' I say. 'Wow.'

'I know. Ugh. It's like the Hamilton of Australia.'

'Could it get any worse?' I regret my words immediately. 'Sorry.'

A shrug. 'Things are undoubtedly shitty.'

I hadn't caught up with all the details and didn't know how to ask. But the short version was that Reece's mum's new husband had fallen off the roof and paralysed himself. This was in Brisbane. He'd been born and raised there and had recently returned home, towing Reece's mum behind him, promising her a better life—or at least a different one. Now he was wrecked, and she had slipped into one of her depressions. Bleak forces had regularly filled Reece's mother's mind when he was growing up, when we all lived up the line a bit. I'd seen glimpses of what it was like for them, right from early on, but I had been too uncomprehending. I just thought she wore her favourite dressing gown unusually often.

When we were fifteen, Reece admitted that he had for years been making—while maintaining that his mum had made them—the best devilled sausages, scalloped potatoes, shepherd's pies, and other one-dish meals that anyone could hope to taste. Each meal would last the two of them nearly a week, unless I stayed over, scoffing down more than my fair share. After Reece's confession, Mum made me cart round casseroles, crumbles, cakes, all sorts—endless smoked-glass dishes brimming with guilt.

'She can't help it,' was about all Reece ever said, when pestered or teased about his mum.

Now he's quit his job, hawked-off his scooter and his belongings, broken his lease, bought a one-way ticket, and who knows when I'll see the bastard again.

Reece looks around his barren room. All there is in here is him, the mirror, the dresser, the bed, and me on the bed with the Kola can. And of course, his bag.

'Seen my banjo?' he says.

'When did you get a banjo?'

'Couple of weeks ago. Maybe a month? From Matt. He got me going, and this rock 'n' roller type in one of the places downstairs—this guy whose genuine last name is Storm—he's taught me a couple of good tricks. But I've mostly been learning songs from tabs and videos online. You know "Wicked Game", the Chris Isaak song?'

'How does it go?'

'It's the one about how the world is on fire and the singer can only be saved by you. Come on, everyone knows that song, Adam.'

'I'm with you. Christ almighty it's a terrible song, though. Why not go for something gutsier, like "Enter Sandman"?'

'Weak selection. But I did start learning it. Sort of mandatory, right?'

'"Wicked Game" is . . .' My mouth hangs open while

I struggle to find the correct term. 'It's an atrocity, an abomination.'

'Objectively not true. Deep down, no human is capable of disliking that song. It works upon us like a law of the universe.'

'Evidently I am not human, or not of this universe,' I say, tapping ash into the Kola can. 'Well, I don't imagine "Spasmolytic" would sound too amazing on banjo.'

'Not too much.'

'Why did Matt give you a banjo, anyway?'

'Sold it to me. He decided he didn't want it, and I decided I wanted it.' Reece flashes me the crack of his pale arse, creeping out from his black skinny jeans, as he searches under the bed. 'Banjo, check.' He drags the banjo out, sits on his knees and rests it on the ground in front of him. Its white body is scratched up, but it has a nice pearl inlay. Fancy for Mutt. Reece nervously fixes his forelock again, then takes up the banjo and picks at the strings, producing a tinny melody.

He begins to sing.

I groan and clamp my hands over my ears, careful not, with the cigarette dangled between my fingers, to singe my hair.

'Such wicked things you do,' Reece says, pretending offence. He stands and leans the banjo against the wall by his bag. Then he turns and throws his hands out. 'And when are *you* going to explore beyond the borders of this fine city?'

'Thought I'd finally try out Dunedin,' I say, playing along, but truthfully. 'Make a move after summer.'

Reece blinks.

'I was going to tell you once it was a bit more of an actual plan, you know?'

'Nice,' he says. 'Get yourself some proper underground culture.'

'Get myself some affordable rent.'

'Get yourself a flashy medical degree and become a world-class surgeon.'

'Well. I talked with Graham. He'll recommend me to some sparkies he knows down there.'

'Get yourself some of the same old shit.'

I suck on my cigarette. 'I could find us a flat.' The words sound limp, because they're essentially a lie—because they betray expected reality. I've never been good at translating my intentions into words, into action. There is a murkiness inside me that will override whatever I think I'm really doing. I should just wish Reece luck and promise to stay in touch, the kind of soft promise grown men make. I'm almost twenty-one, Reece is already there. We are adults, and radical promises can no longer form the basis of an honest friendship.

'Don't make commitments you can't keep,' Reece says. Then, with great sympathy, 'Just as long as you've got the bars with the good music figured out for when we regroup.'

'Will do.' A swirl of nausea forms in my stomach. I swing my legs over the side of the bed, chains rattling around my waist. 'Tell me really, where's this edge you keep talking about?'

'Any direction you please.' Reece grins. I cram the cigarette butt into the mouth of the Kola can and give it a shake, making a dull rattle. 'If you keep going far enough,' he says.

'What about the question of transport?'

'No sweat. I borrowed Matt's car.'

*

My boots skid a little on the pebbles of the beach, and I shudder at the memory of the two idiots from high school who scrambled up the quarried cliffside not far from here. They got pretty high before they slipped, leaving a trail of scoured skin on the stones. One died a few days later, the other was left with a bad limp and some nasty scarring that a dozen new hoodies could never completely hide.

Reece stands near a craggy outcrop of rocks, gripping the banjo by the neck. He sweeps his other hand through the air to indicate the scene before us, the ground beneath us, our arrival at the edge.

We sit and Reece lays the banjo beside him. We haunted the city's beaches in our last years of high school. Mostly the grey stretch of the Petone esplanade, but also, when we needed a drive, we'd come this far, to the southern coast. Wherever it was, clad in black, we'd smoke weed and watch as dusk descended.

'I've been coming here a bit lately,' Reece says. 'I like seeing how the land slips away beneath the water. It's just this quiet and uncertain, but inevitable, end.'

'Yeah,' I say.

'Then you look out to that other line, a bit fuzzy but always there.'

'The horizon?'

'During the day it's this ordinary, steady line in the distance. It changes but never moves, because there's always somewhere else to go. But when the sun sets, it becomes something different. There isn't a name for it.'

I nod, but I don't catch on. I want desperately to understand what Reece is saying.

'Everything seems more strange and lovely when it's been set ablaze,' he says.

The hills around us, the open water, the cloudy sky—they are great planes of messy colour, bleeding into one another. The air is still, though it soon carries the rumble of a boy racer approaching at speed.

'Go drown yourselves, homos,' someone screams above the engine's roar. I twist and see a tricked-out Honda Civic streaking away. A head disappears back inside and a hand emerges, middle finger raised.

'It's the twenty-first century, you cunt,' Reece shouts.

The Civic carries on, around a bend.

'Looked like Craig Button's ride,' I say. 'Sounded like him too.'

'Craig Button, eh. It's a shame someone so handsome has remained such a prick.'

Reece sighs then parts his lips a little and tongues his capped tooth. I wasn't with him when it got chipped three or four years ago. This blitzed skinhead shoved him face-first into a lamp post. Reece would show the tooth off sometimes, a survivor's badge, when he was in the mood for war stories. Still, he quietly saved up the small fortune it cost to get the dental work done. Has he always had this habit of tonguing the tooth?

He rakes his fingers across the banjo strings. 'Do you know how those real-estate psychos described Petone when we were selling Mum's house? They called it "a dream in the making". Jesus. This whole self-important city, at its heart, is as bland and ambitionless as a Briscoes store.'

'Maybe, in the end, that's all most people want.'

Reece turns to look at me. His expression is full of something concealed and frightening, like an eclipsed sun. He opens and closes his mouth, then shakes his head and the expression fades, but the atmosphere has changed. With nowhere else to look, we stare out to sea, where bright colours bloom as if from under the water, from another fire beneath. Behind us, by the houses, a dog yaps then whimpers, falls silent.

'This whole thing is like being chucked backwards in time,' Reece says.

Neither of us says anything else. Something crawls along the base of my spine and I slap at it but strike nothing.

'Thought you'd be around here,' someone says.

I look up to see Mutt coming down from the footpath.

'Heya, Adam,' he says, passing behind me.

I say zip.

Reece moves the banjo to make room for Mutt, who plonks himself down next to Reece and—swiftly, smoothly—wraps an arm around him. Reece stiffens, then relaxes as Mutt gives him a slow squeeze. He turns to face Mutt, then back to the sea. He lays his forearm along Mutt's thigh, tucks his hand behind Mutt's knee.

I also turn to look at the sea.

'I didn't know you guys were together,' I say. Did I know Mutt was queer?

'Better late than never,' Mutt says, and I can't tell whether he means for them, or for telling me.

'Not all long-distance relationships are inherently doomed,' Reece says. 'But to play it safe, Matt's moving to Brisbane as well. In a couple of months.'

'Thinking about it,' Mutt says. 'Need to save some cash.'

My face is hot. I've always thought I'd do anything to make Reece happy. But I have done less and less in the last year or two. Much less, evidently, than Mutt. I have been working loads, falling in with new crowds—sure—but actually, haven't I also been ghosting Reece? I must have been. How else could I have missed this.

'I can loan you some,' I say, startling myself. I badly need a cigarette, but they're in the car. In Mutt's car.

'I might take you up on that,' Mutt says. 'Look. I'm sorry my sister gave you the flick. Bron's brutal with the boys. I know it was ages ago, but it's always felt like a stone between us. Between you and me, I mean. I just wanted to say that.'

Reece smacks me on the hip.

'No hard feelings,' I say. 'Sorry if I exacerbated anything.' I'm unsure what I mean exactly, intending whatever it is for Reece, but Mutt swoops in, taking up my words, my confused intentions, for himself.

'Thanks, Adam. Reece was really unsure how to handle this.'

Reece abruptly picks up the banjo. 'Enough confessions,' he says. 'I'd like to have a pleasant final evening in this godforsaken country. Listen to this.'

He strums the instrument and declares it out of tune but proceeds anyway, warbling excessively, Chris Isaak gone berserk.

Mutt interrupts. 'That's not right.'

'Yes, it is,' Reece says.

'The words are right, but your fingers are wrong.' Mutt leans forwards and nudges Reece's index finger along the fretboard, then lifts and repositions his middle finger. To confirm the new arrangement, he strokes the back of Reece's hand.

'Pluck,' he instructs.

Reece picks the strings and it sounds somehow right where it didn't before. I seethe with happiness for Reece.

'Funny. You barely touched the tuning pegs,' Reece says. 'Let's try this one, then.'

Reece clears his throat. He shifts his fingers, unassisted, then attacks the banjo. A familiar riff erupts, made gutsier by Reece's aggressive handling of the lo-fi instrument. Reece starts thrashing his head, forelock flapping, as the riff goes on, mistakes growing in number but completely ignored.

A ping and a whistle, and Reece shrieks. He flings the banjo away. There is a drop of blood on his cheek.

'Snapped a string,' Matt says.

'I know what happened,' Reece says, an anger in his voice that I haven't heard since high school. 'Take your fucking banjo back.' He shoves it through the pebbly sand towards Matt.

'It's not the banjo's fault.' Matt touches the banjo as tenderly as he had touched Reece a moment before. 'You haven't lost an eye or anything.'

Reece huffs.

'It's been known to happen,' Matt says.

'Lucky me.'

Matt stands, the banjo tucked under his arm. 'Sorry,' he says. 'I'll meet you back at my place. Mum's done a roast.' Matt looks at me, shrugs. 'You can come too, if you want. Bron's not home.'

'No, thanks,' I say. 'You guys might want a quiet night?'

'Whatever. I'll let you say your goodbyes.'

'We've got your car.'

Matt looks at me blankly. 'Yip, and I've got Dad's.'

He stands there like he might say something more, but then just gives the banjo a pat and turns and heads back up the beach.

After a long while, Reece says, 'Matt never actually sold me the banjo. He just loaned it to me. It was something to do together.'

I flinch. While I might have been careless to lose the thread of his story—our story—Reece has been letting it go, as much as he needs to, willingly.

'I'll apologise to him later,' Reece says. Then, 'I'm going to miss you.'

'Likewise,' I say, the swirling nausea in my stomach turning into a storm. My eyes start to sting a moment before the tears come.

Reece shuffles close, puts a hand on my upper arm.

'I'm going to hug you. Just fair warning,' he says, already wrapping his arms around my body. 'Try not to reflexively punch me in the windpipe, but I'm going to kiss you, okay?'

'Lay it on me,' I murmur, and he kisses me by the ear, his forelock scraping my temple.

'You can wipe your face now,' he says, moving back.

I wipe my eyes but leave the kiss. I sniff and a glob of snot hits the back of my throat. I swallow. The end is creeping up, quietly but inevitably. I feel naked and unprepared.

'You'll stay in touch?' I say.

'I'll be lurking on Chat.'

'Choice.' I wipe my nose. 'Give your mum a hug from me.'

'I will. We should get back to the car.'

'I could really do with a smoke.'

We crunch our way across the pebbles, and Reece stops up ahead. He takes a deep, noisy breath and releases it. 'This is all we've got,' he says, waving a hand around vaguely. 'Apart from this, not a thing. You'd feel better, and smell nicer, you know, if you quit the cigs.'

I want to ask whether he means apart from all we've got, or apart from the knowledge of all we've got, we have nothing. But it's a hopeless question.

Reece steps onto the footpath, and I stand still, the stony ground shifting under me, the air around us already turning grey and cool.

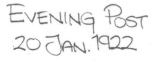

EVENING POST
20 JAN. 1922

A MIDSUMMER NIGHT'S DRAMA

—◆—

ACTOR'S FIERY REVENGE OVER CASTING SLIGHT

A fire that broke out overnight has destroyed the Wellington Repertory Society Theatre. Four of the Society's members were present, making final preparations for to-night's scheduled opening of William Shakespeare's "A Midsummer Night's Dream." Stage manager Mr. M. Smith said that by the time they noticed black smoke entering backstage the fire had already engulfed the stalls. He described their escape as lucky. Fire fighters battled the blaze for several hours, however nothing of the interior could be saved.

Police are treating the fire as suspicious after it was discovered that one of the actors, Mr. R. Harris, failed to report to work this morning at the shoe retailer where he has been employed. A subsequent search of Mr. Harris's home uncovered signs of a hasty departure.

Mr. Smith said that in recent weeks Mr. Harris had appeared increasingly agitated. Having played the titular role in "King Lear" last summer, Mr. Harris had complained openly that he saw his casting in the role of Bottom in this year's production as an "insulting demotion to a barmy character of little substance."

Concerns over Mr. Harris's mental fitness had been raised only facetiously, Mr. Smith said. The show's director, Mrs. A. Ford, has admitted that such concerns should perhaps have been taken more seriously.

Vowing that the show must go on, Mrs. Ford has announced that the production will be relocated to a venue on Tory Street. Mrs. Ford herself will play the part of Bottom, appearing in mock-beard. The season will be delayed by a fortnight while members of the Society reconstruct set pieces and source replacements for the various props and costumes consumed by the fire.

On behalf of the Society, Mrs. Ford has thanked the community for their continued support. She said, "Whilst events in our staging of this famous Comedy have taken a turn towards Tragedy, we will restore matters to their proper order." She added, "You never can tell what twists and turns life might take. Alas, we must learn to work with the impromptu script that we're supplied."

The Universe for Beginners

Scotty closed the front door gently behind him, the click of the lock's tongue nearly inaudible. It was dark and silent in the apartment except for the shifting glow and low murmur from the television tucked out of sight in the living room at the end of the hallway. He took a few cautious steps forwards, then paused to ease open Māia's bedroom door. Peering inside, he could make out his daughter's sleeping form and hear her soft breathing. She slept in the depths of space, glow-in-the-dark stars and planets strewn across the ceiling and walls. He left her to her dreaming and crept further along the hallway.

'Mum?' he whispered. 'You awake?'

His mother, Eve, had one arm draped along the back of the couch. Her hand, poking out from a woollen sleeve, loosely grasped the television remote. Moving closer, Scotty caught the fluttering sound of her snoring. On the television, a late-night news host laughed in quiet gasps under the studio lights.

'Mum,' Scotty whispered again. The snoring continued. He slipped the remote from her hand and turned off the television.

'Oh!' Eve's body snapped upright. 'Is that you, son? I was just resting my eyes.'

'Sorry. Things ran later than I'd hoped.'

'Not a bother,' she said, rubbing her eyes with the heels

of her hands.

Scotty adjusted the dimmer to turn on the lights—not too bright. 'How are you doing?'

'Kei te pai. And you?'

'Knackered. Work was a real slog. Māia was no trouble?'

'Not at all. She's a little angel. I'm the one who likes to make mischief.'

Scotty saw Eve glance at the clock on the kitchen wall. It was nearly twenty minutes past ten. He moved through the living room, straight to the fridge.

'Did she get her homework done?'

'Absolutely,' Eve said. 'After a quick game.'

'Mum.'

'Only half an hour or so. I liked watching. She was growing things on another planet and fighting men in spacesuits.'

'*Red World War?*'

'Hm. I think that was the name.'

'Yeah. She's pretty good at strategy.'

Scotty removed a snap-lock container from the fridge and spooned egg salad into a bowl. It had been his favourite dish since he was a young boy, and although it had been made for him many times by different people, it only ever tasted right when his mother made it—following a recipe that only she knew. It seemed fateful to Scotty, in hindsight, that Māia's mother, Janine, couldn't stomach the taste of mayonnaise and egg combined. He'd felt victorious when, two or three years after he and Janine separated, Māia also declared her love for her nana's egg salad. That was back when Māia still lived with Janine. These days, Eve made the dish almost every time she visited Scotty and Māia at their apartment.

Scotty returned to the living room with his bowl and a fork. He sat on the couch beside his mother and started eating.

'How did it go?' Eve waved her hand in the air. 'The launch?'

'It was fine.'

'Don't speak with your mouth full.'

'Sorry, Mum.' Scotty swallowed. 'I'm starving.'

'She'll get bad habits with a father like you.'

'She keeps me in line. You know we launched a website, not a rocket?'

'I know this much—she's got your smarts, my mokopuna.'

Scotty ran his tongue over a speck of parsley in his teeth. 'Sorry we haven't seen you as much lately.'

'Oh? I don't keep track of such things.'

'Yeah, right.'

He spotted something dark on the far side of the coffee table, hunched low to the ground. Eve's overnight bag. Scotty sighed. He couldn't call his mother a taxi—not after she'd stayed so late and come prepared. And especially not since Māia would have seen Eve's bag and would be anticipating a nice morning with her nana. He should be thankful for Eve's presence, and for her help. It wasn't the end of the world if she stayed—only the end of an already long week.

'Got everything you need for the morning?' he said.

Eve winked. 'Āe, son.'

Scotty stood and took his bowl to the kitchen, then returned to collect Eve's bag. He nodded towards the hallway, to his bedroom. 'I'll chuck on some fresh sheets.'

'I'll give you a hand.'

'It is, yes—a very lovely morning,' Scotty heard a woman say. The voice seemed at a distance—both real and an effect of the thick sleep he was emerging from. It wasn't Māia's voice, or Eve's.

'I think he might still be sleeping,' he heard his mother say, a little louder than was natural.

The words *see you Saturday* surged up from Scotty's subconscious, jolting him completely awake. He threw aside the blanket and pushed himself up with one arm. His back spasmed and he groaned and flopped back down. Moving carefully, he rolled onto his side, levered himself up and twisted around to look. The front door was open. Standing in a bright rectangle of morning light was Sally with her boy Samuel—and Eve.

Eve looked down the hallway at Scotty. 'Mōrena,' she said.

'Mōrena,' Scotty replied, keeping his voice down. Then, 'Hello, Sally. Hey, Sam.'

He got up from the couch, glad he'd slept in a T-shirt and track pants, and stretched his back, unkinking it with three loud pops. He made his way down the hallway and stood at the threshold behind his mother.

'Sorry if this is bad timing,' Sally said. She had the strap of a nylon bag over one shoulder. 'Are you all right? You sounded like you were in pain.'

'No. No, no. Not at all,' Scotty said. 'Come in. Please, come in.'

'Shoes,' Sally said to Sam.

She and Sam placed their shoes with Scotty's and Eve's, next to the rack piled up with Māia's footwear.

'I was about to make some bacon and mushrooms,' Eve said. 'Plenty to go around.'

'It's okay, thank you. We already ate,' Sally said. 'We can come back a bit later?'

'I was just about to get ready,' Scotty said. 'Overslept, sorry.'

'Sam was up early, weren't you?' Sally said, looking down at her son. 'He's acting shy, but he's excited. We brought a few things to contribute for lunch.'

Eve accepted the nylon bag from Sally.

'I'll leave you to chat while I cook some kai,' Eve said. She raised her eyebrows with the merest flicker, then headed down the hall.

'Coffee? Tea?' Scotty said. 'What would you like to drink, Sam? I'll wake Māia up.'

'Māia!' Sam said.

'Sam—Scotty asked if you'd like a drink,' Sally said.

'Juice,' Sam said. 'Please.'

'I'll have coffee, please,' Sally said, then quieter, 'I didn't expect to meet your mother like this.'

'I didn't forget,' Scotty replied. 'I had a work thing last night and Mum was watching Māia. I didn't forget.'

Scotty watched Sally and Sam wander towards the living room, then he opened Māia's bedroom door. She stepped back from the spot where she had been listening.

'You totally did forget,' she said. 'You're hopeless.'

Scotty moved aside and Māia edged past him, clutching her clothes, with a towel draped over one arm. She was only twelve and already Scotty worried about the years to come.

'Hi, ratbag! Hi, Sally,' she said.

'Mōrena, angel,' Eve said.

'Mōrena, Nana! Make sure Dad doesn't touch my bacon.'

'Better be quick then,' Scotty called out. 'My tummy's rumbling.'

*

Sally and Māia sat in the back seat with Sam between them. As he drove, Scotty developed a habit of looking now and then in the rear-view mirror at Sally, then across at Eve in the front passenger seat.

'You're sure it's no trouble I come along?' Eve said.

'Nana,' Māia said from the back, 'nau mai. You're always welcome.'

'You just love me for my cooking,' Eve said.

'We-e-e-ll, love is love,' Māia said.

'Oh,' Eve said, 'I'm right, am I?'

'Jokes,' Māia said.

'Jokes,' Sam mimicked. 'Jokes!'

Scotty pulled into the parking lot at the top of the hill, beside the terminus of the cable car that ran between the Botanic Garden and Lambton Quay. They walked the short distance to the lookout and watched as cloud shadows played across the harbour, then weaved their way along the tar-seal path to their destination—the observatory, Māia's pick.

Nearing the ticket desk, Scotty offered to pay for everyone.

'Don't be silly,' Sally said. 'We can split.'

'There's one extra on my side.'

'Let's go halves,' Sally said, and turned to the man at the counter. 'Family pass, plus one senior? Split it down the middle, please.'

'Hello, Scotty,' the man said. He looked at Sally. 'You're familiar.'

'Do I know you?' Sally said.

'Ashton. He's in 4D,' Scotty explained, as Sally swiped her credit card. 'This is Sally. She's in 1C.'

'The apartments,' Sally said, and shook her head. 'For goodness' sake.'

'Small world.' Ashton grinned, then put through Scotty's half of the transaction. 'And how's the interstellar girl?'

'Rocketing along, as ever,' Scotty said.

'You know, a new planetarium show's being polished up. A sneak preview could be in the offing—on the house. I could keep a few spots open?'

'I'm sure she'd love that. Thank you. Wouldn't Sam enjoy that?'

'It's very generous,' Sally said. 'Are you sure?'

'No problem.' Ashton handed over their tickets, then waved across at Māia and Sam, who waved back. 'I'd better let you get on with your morning.'

'Seems like friendly service,' Eve said to Scotty, as they moved away.

'Yeah. Nice bloke,' Scotty said, stuffing the tickets into his jacket pocket.

Māia quickly took the lead, with Sam close behind and the three adults trailing.

'*Ritual of retelling . . .*' Māia began reading out loud, unseen, her voice coming from beyond the place where two walls curved together into short, nested spirals, forming the narrow entrance to the museum's permanent exhibition.

The construction of the entrance meant you had to turn through a tight arc as you passed through, as though spinning forwards, as though being born.

Scotty let Eve and Sally go ahead. When he entered, Māia had already finished reading and moved on. She was showing Sam the large, clear tubes that reached the ceiling and were packed with grains of sand that, as she explained, were still, incredibly, fewer in number than all the stars in the sky.

On the wall where Māia had been reading, the text was positioned at a height that invited the attention of children, anyone from Sam's age up to Māia's. The font was too small to be read from where Scotty stood. Even so, the lines came easily into his mind: *Every time the creation story is retold, the Universe is brought forth from the void once more.*

He knew these words by heart, having passed through this gap between the two walls countless times, with Māia always rushing ahead, reading the words aloud. Along the wall to the left, the universe unfurled from the seed of the Big Bang. Along the wall to the right unfurled the story that starts with the parentless Io-matua-te-kore: *In Io was the potential for everything in the Universe.*

There were other ways to enter the exhibition, but they always began at this point—the beginning of the universe.

Eve was standing where Māia had been a minute earlier, appraising the rightward wall, reading the words, bent forwards to see better.

There is no end to the story, because creation never stops becoming. There is always a new generation waiting to add the next lines to the story.

Scotty saw Māia as proof of that. He saw her as the kind of becoming that he feared he hadn't been for his mother. There was a broad movement to Māia's life that he recognised from his own—the movement away from a parent then back again. Although, Māia had never completely left Scotty—he and Janine had always shared custody. Still did, in theory. Whereas Scotty and his brothers had been taken away from Eve. Had been placed into foster care, because the state said that it would be safer. That the children couldn't be kept together. Eve had been left to endure the violence of her husband until, years later, he went into one last drunken rage, put one last hole in the living-room wall, and his heart failed him for good. Many of Scotty's memories of his father were hazy—he'd been so young when he went away, that sharp start to a slow and sorry letting go. He hadn't been there to witness the changes in his father's face that night, but he had imagined it many times—the man's sour-milk complexion, webbed with inflamed capillaries, turning at last a dull and chilly blue.

Ahead, Māia and Sam were playing at the gravity well, supervised by Sally. They sent coloured bouncy balls rolling across bright nebulae and constellations, the balls circling one another in wild orbits as they spiralled towards the curved funnel's centre, which narrowed into darkness—a black hole. The balls circled quicker and quicker towards it, then one after another finally vanished.

Scotty put a hand out, bracing against the Big Bang.

Māia knew her grandfather had been troubled and had caused her grandmother pain. She knew that, because of him, Scotty and his brothers did not see their mother for a long time. For Scotty, not until he'd almost finished high school. He wondered if Māia ever wished she'd had the chance to meet her grandfather, to discover for herself something of his human dimensions. She'd once met Bill and Carol, who had provided Scotty with his final foster home. He had stopped receiving Christmas cards from 'B + C' by then, but Māia was insistent. It had been a short visit, a ticklish afternoon tea during a tour north one summer holiday, the ageing couple still busy with their rosters of children. Was it wrong that his daughter had met Bill but neither of her grandfathers? Scotty thought Janine's dad had died of cancer, but he couldn't say for sure which kind. He'd been young, though—gone before Janine had finished high school. Dead like Scotty's dad. Dead years before any of his children had children of their own.

Eve was touching Scotty's arm. She was asking if he was all right.

Scotty let out a long breath.

'Good, Mum. Tired still, I guess.' He wanted to say, *I had this feeling of falling inwards*. Instead, he said, 'Got lost in my thoughts.'

Sally approached them.

'I think they could keep going at that for hours,' she said. 'Māia says you two come here a lot.'

'She's keen on space. Reckons she'll be the first human to set foot on Mars. Big dreams for a twelve-year-old, eh?'

'She's a sharp girl,' Eve said.

'Sam loves space too,' Sally said. 'He's sure he'll make contact with aliens one day.'

'Māia will teach him a thing or two,' Eve said. 'Looks like they're getting along together.'

'Yes. It's nice to see,' Sally said.

'He's your only one?' Eve said.

'Mum,' Scotty said.

'It's just a question.'

'It's okay. Yes, Sam's it.'

'I'm not prying.'

'I don't mind,' Sally said, as Sam came towards them, walking pigeon-toed. 'What's the matter?'

'Need to pee,' Sam said.

'Back in a minute,' Sally said. They disappeared down a tunnel painted black and latticed with glowing strips of neon green.

Scotty and Eve watched Māia as she sent bouncy balls spiralling once more through space. There were a few other families that Scotty could see wandering the exhibitions. He noticed they were mostly fathers and sons. It wasn't always like that, but often it was, and Scotty wondered if they were single fathers too.

There was that word—*too*. But Scotty was dating Sally, so he wasn't exactly single. Though he wasn't entirely with Sally, either. They weren't *together*. Being together was something bigger. Between dating and being together was a long stretch of—what exactly?

'She seems nice,' Eve said.

'Yeah, Sally's good,' Scotty said. 'She's great.'

'You look happy around her. I like to see it . . .' Eve's voice seemed to fold back on itself. Scotty thought he knew what she'd been about to say—to ask.

'I'm sorry I hadn't told you. We're just taking things slowly, trying to be cautious. For the kids, for ourselves.'

'I understand.'

'I wanted to be sure first, to save the disappointment if it didn't work out.'

'She looks quite sure, if you ask me. Convenient arrangement, too.'

'How do you mean?'

'Living in the same building.'

'Sally told you?'

'Āe. When we were putting lunch together. You leave two wāhine alone, we'll kōrero about all sorts of things.'

'It's not like I'm knocking on her door every night.'

'Don't worry,' Eve said, chuckling. 'She didn't say much about all that.'

Scotty blushed, but he was glad Eve and Sally could be friendly.

'You know what I like most about her?' he said. 'How she is with Māia, and with Sam. She's good with them.'

'As are you.'

Māia returned the bouncy balls to their holder beneath the gravity well. She came over and announced she was going to capture satellites.

'All right, dynamo,' Scotty said, and they followed her to a low door that led into a room Scotty knew to be decorated like a space-shuttle pod. Grey panelled walls, survival props and a videogame console that Māia would sit in front of for as long as he'd let her.

'I feel like I'm just guessing my way through all this,' Scotty said.

'Nobody has all the answers.' Eve pointed at a man with a baby strapped to his chest and a boy leading him by the hand. 'You can bet he's making it up as well. We all do what we can.'

'Māia has this points system. I get a point every time I do something dumb. The points I'll be getting today! She makes me buy her something when I've racked up enough,' Scotty paused. 'It started as a joke. I still don't know how she counts them up. Sometimes it's like—'

'She told me about the points,' Eve said. Scotty frowned. 'A while ago, when I asked where she gets all her shoes. She likes being with you. Not just because of the shoes.'

'I really don't know. I try.'

'Watching you be a father to her, it makes me think about back then. When you were a boy.'

'Mum—'

'And your brothers.'

'Mum, you don't have to keep going there.'

'I don't go there, son. It stays with me.'

'Yeah. I know.' Eve sniffed, and Scotty searched his pockets but found nothing that he could offer her, only their entry tickets. 'Same here.'

Eve fished a tissue from her handbag. 'There's so much I wish I could have done for you. For all my boys.'

Scotty moved as if to touch Eve but tucked his hands back into his jacket.

'Have you heard from your brothers?'

'Sure.' Scotty hesitated. 'I called and spoke to Joel a few weeks ago. He says he's doing okay.'

'Is he?'

'I think so.' Scotty recalled his eldest brother's voice— quiet in a way that could have meant many things. 'He's getting there.'

Eve wiped at her eyes again, then returned the tissue to her handbag. 'We should talk about something else. I don't want to look a mess in front of your new friend. Is she— ka mōhio rānei ia? Does she know?'

'Just the main stuff. Not the details about how things happened.'

Eve nodded.

Scotty swallowed hard, taking the truth down into his gut. The truth was, he and Sally had talked more, one time. He hadn't said much, but it was enough. Sally had said that she felt awed by his mother, in a sense, and Scotty hadn't known how to take that, hadn't been able to ask what she meant. He had sat there silently in Sally's apartment, with that feeling of falling inwards, leaving Sally to apologise and change the subject. Even with Janine still hovering in Scotty's mind—the demands she'd made to know more, for him to be able to give her more, to give their relationship more—he had realised that night with Sally that, as little as he had said, he should have waited longer to say it.

'Māia really enjoys being around you,' he said to Eve. 'You give her this real energy. After we see you, she's all *Nana this* and *Nana that.* Have I told you that?'

Eve cleared her throat. 'What's happening with Māia's mother? Is she still moving overseas?'

'Yeah. She's getting married in Chile in November.'

'She knows you're seeing someone?'

'Kāo. Janine doesn't care, not really.'

'I know it's been tough, son. But she cares for her daughter. How will they keep in touch?'

'She said she'd come back and visit early next year. Then Māia could go to Chile for a few weeks the year after. Janine's happy to cover half the airfares. Which still leaves the other bloody half, of course. But there's Skype.'

'Things will look up. Little by little, you'll see.'

'Sure. I just don't want Janine to become a bad memory for her, you know? I don't want to become one either.'

'Nobody ever wants that. Your daughter doesn't hold anything against you. It's good you're having another go, starting again.' Eve looked over Scotty's shoulder. 'I could take care of the tamariki tonight.'

'Hm?'

'I can watch them at your place.' Eve was whispering. 'You two can take off, have some time to yourselves.'

'Sorry we were longer than expected,' Sally said, coming up alongside Scotty.

'Found you,' Sam said, tapping Scotty's leg. 'Where's Māia?'

'Oh. She's taking a drive through space.' Scotty pointed towards the low door.

'Hold on. I thought you were hungry?' Sally said, gently taking Sam's arm. She looked at Scotty. 'I'm not interrupting?'

'No, no. We were just chatting,' Scotty said. 'You're

hungry, Sam? I guess it must be about time for lunch.' He looked at his watch. 'Maybe an early one.'

'I'll get Māia,' Eve said, and she went across to the shuttle-pod room and peered inside.

At the Rose Garden, they arranged themselves around a picnic table and unpacked the lunch that Eve and Sally had made. Eve prompted Māia to give the karakia kai. Looking at the food in front of them, Scotty said, 'I'm a little more peckish than I'd thought—let's tuck in.' There were cut sandwiches, bananas and mandarins, muesli bars and biscuits, a thermos of hot tea, a bottle of orange juice and another of water.

After they'd all finished eating, Scotty reached into the chilly bin for cups and milk for the tea, and discovered the snap-lock container with the last of the egg salad.

'Anyone else keen?' he asked.

'I'm stuffed,' Māia said, rubbing her stomach.

Sam took a break from running around the picnic table and rubbed his belly too, shouting, 'Stuffed! Stuffed!'

'Oi—Samuel, enough of that,' Sally said. Then, to Scotty, 'Yes, please. I'd love a try.'

Scotty split the serving between them. After Sally had devoured a couple of forkfuls, Eve said to her, 'Good kai?'

'Really good,' Sally said, and picked parsley from between her front teeth. 'I haven't eaten egg salad in forever.'

'Can I have some?' said Sam.

'You told me you were full.'

'Found room,' he said, poking his side with a finger.

'It's all finished, sorry. Have a shortbread if you like,' Sally said.

Sam scarcely chewed before swallowing, washing the

lumps of biscuit down with more juice from the cup that Sally handed to him.

'I'll make extra next time, to go around,' Eve said.

'What's in it?' Sally asked.

'Oh, eggs and mayonnaise, salt and pepper, a few fresh herbs. The secret's in how you combine it all together.'

'Not even I know the recipe,' Scotty said. 'I've asked a hundred times.'

'Samuel, sit down a minute, please. Give your lunch a chance to settle,' Sally said.

Sam was walking quickly back and forth along the grass verge that marked the boundary of a garden plot, balancing with his arms held out. He stopped suddenly and made a gulping sound, then vomited a stream of food and orange juice at the base of a starkly budless rose bush.

'Gross!' Māia said. 'You little spew bomb.'

'Samuel!' Sally said. 'Watch your top, please. Come here. I told you to settle down.'

'At least he has good aim,' Scotty said, and handed Sally a small stack of serviettes. 'By and large.'

While Sally cleaned Sam up and carried him to the car, Scotty and Māia and Eve packed up the picnic gear. Māia took Scotty's keys and shut the gear in the boot.

Eve indicated the place where Sam had been sick. 'We should take care of that.'

'Oh, right.' Scotty dug the toe of his shoe into the soft soil and flicked it over the vomit until it was covered, then he and Eve rejoined the others in the car.

Scotty was thankful for the flatter route out of the Rose Garden, avoiding the winding roads they'd taken from the other direction earlier. He plotted a course through downtown that had, he thought, fewer traffic lights, heading towards the apartment block beyond the central city's southern boundary.

'Is everything still okay back there?' he asked. 'Won't be too long.'

'Stinks of spew,' Māia said. 'Open the windows some more?'

'We're okay,' Sally said, checking Sam's sleeping face. 'Just ate too much is all. And got a bit overexcited.'

Māia was the first out of the car once Scotty had parked behind their building. She loudly sucked in a lungful of air. Sally slid across the back seat and slipped out through Māia's open door, then went around to collect Sam.

Inside, Eve and Māia climbed into the elevator and headed for the apartment above, taking the picnic gear with them, while Scotty went with Sally and Sam to their place on the ground floor.

Outside her front door, Sally said, 'Sorry for the bad end.'

'Can't be helped,' Scotty said. 'Mum offered to take the kids for the night. Maybe another time?'

'That'd be neat.' She kissed Scotty on the cheek. 'Have you ever met Liv and George? Retired couple, right next door there. They've looked after Sam before. They might be okay looking after both of them, every now and then.'

'Mum really won't mind,' Scotty said. 'But good to have options.'

Sam let out a moan.

'Text you later,' Sally said, then jiggled her keys in the lock and disappeared inside with her son.

Scotty entered the stairwell. The elevator was not much quicker than taking the stairs, after waiting for the cab to descend then the slow grinding upwards. And Scotty liked the stairs. They brought him into himself, allowing him to move under his own power, at his own pace. He paused at the next landing. Had Sally meant to suggest that her neighbours babysit the children instead of Eve? Sally had enjoyed the day, and Eve's company, hadn't she? Why wouldn't she want Eve to stay involved? Scotty replayed Sally's voice, looking for something in her tone that might confirm her intentions—either a reaction against the true circumference of his life, or an attempt to expand it.

An ache struck at Scotty's temples. He waited three long breaths then continued up the stairs.

Eve opened the door to the apartment when he knocked.

'How about a cup of tea before you take this kuia home?'

'Sure,' Scotty said. He followed his mother to the living room.

'Turn that off,' he said to Māia, who had loaded up a saved game of *Red World War.* Beams of light were streaking across the television screen while she sat lost in a dream of the future.

'Oh, it's just a little fun, nē?' Eve said. 'Give her half an hour. We'll have a cuppa and a little rest.'

'Sure.'

Eve began fussing with the kettle and mugs. She smiled at Scotty, and he saw that something was resonating, still singing within her, a string plucked and a note held. He saw, too, in the slight tremble of her bottom lip, that she felt as tired as he did.

A little rest. A little fun.

Little by little, things will look up, his mother had said.

Well, maybe the world depended on little things. Big things happened, of course—they came crashing through lives all the time. But weren't big things made from little things? Little by little, couldn't things get worse, just the same as they could get better? Little by little, you might not even notice it. The little things could be relentless like that and—and the kettle boiled then—

—and Scotty told Eve to take a seat, he'd finish making the tea.

They Always Come for the Sweet Things

Dark beady strands droop down from the seams in the kitchen wallpaper towards the linoleum floor. They resemble tiny drops of opaque resin that have run together into chains then gradually hardened in the air. Without getting too close, the boy sees that the densest segments are those nearest the points in the walls where the droplets emerged. He sees that these segments are still slowly moving. The boy turns his head left and right, up and down, taking in the sight of them all. He was forewarned, but he didn't know exactly what to picture. This is far worse than he could have imagined.

A mass breaks away from a patch of wallpaper beside the sink and strikes the benchtop, at the boy's eye level.

'Mum,' he shouts. 'Mum—Mum—Mum—Mum!'

'What? What's wrong?' his mum asks, rushing down the hallway from the apartment's entrance and into the small living room adjacent to the kitchen. She sets her bags of groceries down on the coffee table. 'Is it the ants? Are there many?' Her eyes move to where her son is looking, above the sink. 'Oh, bloody Nora! Look at them all. Go and grab the vacuum cleaner, will you, please? I said, can you please go and get—oi! Listen to me. Get the vacuum, please.'

Ants tickle when they crawl over his skin, when he's playing on the cracked concrete veranda out front or in the car park at the rear of the apartment block, when he can sneak away that far. Those ants never feel sticky, not even when he crushes them under his thumb. Maybe the ants in the kitchen secreted a special substance when they were dying, causing them to clump together and droop from the walls like this. The poison might have triggered a chemical reaction in their bodies. Or maybe the ants linked their legs together—if they had figured out what was happening to them, they might have then turned to help or hold each other. The ants outside sometimes did that, joining their bodies together in warfare or in work. But some of the ants in the kitchen are separate from the rest and died alone. He notices the ants on the sand-coloured linoleum, like crumbs of burnt mince spat from the pan, still slick with cooking oil, but full of poison.

'Would you get the bloody vacuum cleaner, please?'

The boy nods. With his head tilted groundward, looking out for more of the tiny, curled corpses, he walks past his mum's feet, past the couch at the edge of the living room, past the oversized potted cactus. He makes his way down the hallway, stopping just beyond the Cabinet of Precious Objects. He tugs open the door to the storage closet and peeks inside. The contraption, with its extendable tubing and hose and attachments, looms like an enormous, malformed stick insect. The boy is brave and when he squints through one eye he can see the vacuum cleaner for what it really is—a collection of insensible plastic and steel. Still, it's bigger than him and he has trouble manoeuvring its parts free of the cardboard boxes of Christmas decorations, and the sealed plastic bins of photo albums no longer browsed and old letters no longer read. He bumps the sucking end of the metal tube against the Cabinet of Precious Objects, causing it to rattle. He swings back away from the cabinet and some unseen part of the vacuum scrapes the opposite wall of the hallway, leaving a dark scuff mark.

Somehow, his mum manages this task without incident every Sunday. Though, she is much bigger than the vacuum cleaner—she can wrap her arms around it, hold all the parts together, keep them under control. He'll watch her do it, then follow her as she moves from room to room. He'll try to catch the cat's tail as it scarpers past them, away from the noise. 'If you want to help,' his mum will say, 'grab a rag and start dusting.' And he does, working the rag carefully over the dressers in both of their bedrooms, and the coffee table, and the other places he can reach. He would help more, but he's still too little for most chores. Dusting low surfaces and washing the bottom half of the car are his lot. His mum has her job at the supermarket, and each day when she gets home, after collecting him from school, there are the piles of washing, dinner to cook, lunch to prepare, dishes to wash. And every Sunday, the housework.

He stays with his dad every second weekend in a flat across town, a place no larger than his mum's apartment, though his dad never seems busy with housework of his own. The two of them spend their weekends together watching cartoons and throwing the Frisbee around the park.

Of course, his mum watches television with him too. Usually animated movies on DVD—like his favourite, *Tarzan*, which they act out on wild days, indulging their inner animal, though always minding, please, the furniture. And they can play card games—Go Fish, Snap, Memory— for whole afternoons. But his mum always misses the earliest and best of the weekend cartoons, because the boy knows not to wake her. Another hour, a few more zees, till the little hand is on the eight, a bit longer, please, till the little hand's on the nine.

The apartment he and his mum share is much smaller than the house they used to live in. They stayed on for a time after his dad moved out. 'We have to sell this place, so Daddy can take his half and we can take ours. That way everybody gets less than they deserve and that's called being fair,' his mum explained, her eyes red. Then, hugging him, she said, 'I'm sorry. Sometimes adults say things they shouldn't, even Mummy and Daddy.' Chores could take a whole weekend with the house, even when his dad was still there to help. Leaves on the lawn to be raked up, muck in the roof gutters to be scooped out, ashes to be swept carefully from the fireplace. And there just weren't enough hours in a day, after his dad left, to plaster and paint the cracks in the walls, to replace the worn carpet, to put new boards on the deck where the old ones had rotted. Only so much could be done before the FOR SALE sign went up. 'That'll drive the bloody price down,' his mum said. 'But so what? Less for everyone.'

The boy has an idea that the apartment is still too big for his mum, even though there's no grass that needs mowing, no driveway slick with moss to be water-blasted away, no veggie patch overtaken with endless weeds.

Since moving into the apartment, there have been special guests, visiting one at a time, who have helped his mum wash the dishes after she's made the three of them dinner from one of her fancy recipes—groceries all specially bought, and not a crumb of burnt mince in sight. Some guests have tried saving his mum the effort of cooking and washing up by ordering Chinese takeaways or pizza. But even then, they wear eager grins when she says 'I hope you boys saved room for dessert' as she stands at the boundary between the living room and kitchen, already clutching bowls of ice cream skewered at angles with spoons.

While some guests have gone on to stay the night, none have ever offered to help with the housework in the morning. One of them—the most recent, whose visits have become more frequent than any guest before him—has started to join the boy in watching the early cartoons. They curl up at either end of the couch in dressing gowns—the boy in his own, the guest in his mum's—with cups of hot chocolate warming their hands, laughing as quietly as they can, waiting for the boy's mum to join them. Yet even this guest will depart for his own apartment on one of the floors above before it's time to drag the vacuum cleaner from its hallway den.

The body of the vacuum cleaner bangs against the hallway skirting as the boy hauls it behind him. He ignores that terrible noise and charges ahead, past the potted cactus and the couch, into the kitchen. His mum is crouched in front of the oven with her arms clamped against its sides, like she and the oven are engaged in a wrestling deadlock and it's anyone's game. She grunts and heaves the oven forwards with two lurching thuds. Then she stands and peers into the shadowy void behind.

'They're bloody everywhere!'

'Is this gonna be the end?' the boy asks.

'The end of what? Bring the vacuum over here, please.'

'Are the ants all gone now?'

His mum wipes a hand across her forehead. 'Well, there are a lot of ants out there,' she says, gesturing towards the kitchen wall. He understands she means that the ants exist in the world beyond the apartment. But he also understands that the kitchen wall and the outside are connected, such that even when he and his mum are standing inside their apartment, they're still standing in the same world as the ants, and these realities will always be entangled.

A cluster of resinous bodies falls from the light fitting in the kitchen's ceiling and ruptures on the floor. The boy and his mum jump with fright, then stare up at the source.

'Bloody hell. Can you plug the vacuum in, please?'

The boy's eyes remain fixed on the ceiling, searching the whole of its cracked surface, the loose light fitting, the slender spaces along the edges of the cornice, trying to assess the extent of the connectedness between the world of the ants and their own.

'Can you—oi! I need you to plug the vacuum cleaner in.'

'Mum. The upstairs people.'

'Never mind the upstairs people.'

'The ants will get them too.'

'Would you plug the vacuum in, please?'

He drops his eyes to the vacuum cleaner, then grabs the cord and drags it across the linoleum, then across the carpet, and plugs it into a socket beneath the television. The vacuum starts up right away and the cat leaps from the couch and escapes down the hallway.

'You need to keep the cat bowl clean,' his mum says, raising her voice above the noise. She uses the exposed end of the long metal tube to target swatches of bodies around the cat's food bowl and the rubbish bin. Strings of dead ants rise up as if mounting a counter-attack, before disappearing into the tube's mouth.

'It's expensive getting an exterminator around,' his mum shouts, as hundreds more vanish from existence. 'The ants only come inside if there's food to attract them. That cat bowl is disgusting. You need to rinse it every day. And keep the sugar in the fridge. The ants always come for the sweet things.'

Provided with Eyes, Thou Departest

His wife washed up over and over again on the lakeshore. Grey as a pool of mercury, the lake sat in a meteoric crater at the top of a high mountain. A long, difficult tramp to reach the access point: a day, two days, a week. Then, no proper track down from the ridgeline, or none that was adequately maintained. Thick bush, streamers of supplejack tugging at his limbs, branches scraping his hands and his face. Finally, the bush gave way to brambles that reached across a narrow shoreline of rock to stroke the lake's edge. He stood for a long time each time, just gazing at the broad body of water. Oddly unreflective, as blank as a damaged mind. Its surface was, each time, eventually disrupted when, like a trail of tree-fall debris, sitting low in the water, the separate parts of her drifted towards him, guided by some unseen current. A detached and pearlescent thigh. A forearm dipping below the waterline at the elbow and the fingers rising above, curled as though holding an invisible crook. Her downturned head, the copper hair fanning out in a fibrous clot. All of her washing up on the stony shore, coming to rest, piece by piece, at his bare and bloodied feet.

He lay still awhile then rose from his bed, the duvet tossed aside in his sleep. Out on the front porch—a space clogged with pots of sagging shrubs and ferns, and hanging baskets overflowing with shoots and fronds but few flowers—he stood looking out from the shadowy fringe of suburbia. Their battered weatherboard house, perched on a scrubby rise, had lasted the passage of a hundred years. The city lay below, arranged like a rock garden strung with chintzy lights, beside the pond of the harbour.

He picked at the thick staple on the handrail that the real estate agent had left behind. Only half embedded but stuck fast in the wood. The agent must have sliced the corrugated plastic away around it. Perhaps they'd left the staple on purpose, hoping that in some trivial but persistent way it would irritate the homeowner who'd withdrawn from the market and denied the agent their commission. He knew there must be places he could go, even some place down there—underneath one of the rocks of the city. Somewhere cheap and manageable. Somewhere that was somewhere else. He eyed the array of potted flora around him. There was too much that he would have to shift or sell or throw away. It was not possible.

He wiped his eyes with his thumbs then turned his mind to the day ahead, to the lesson plans he hadn't written, the lesson plans he would just copy over. Nothing new under the sun.

Aidan Jackson and James Gilroy from Physical Education were in his corner, talking and laughing gruffly, slapping each other on the back. The seats all cracked brown vinyl and flaky chrome plating—were arranged around the perimeter of the staffroom, as though for a large therapy group. Bryce spotted a vacant section beyond the low tables scattered with newsletters. He swung past the tables, mug of tea in one hand, sandwich in the other, current issue of *New Zealand Geographic* clamped under an armpit.

He tucked the tea away under his seat and put the magazine on his lap, then tackled the clingwrap on his sandwich. Half of it was squished flat, soggy with mayonnaise, which had also found its way into the folds of the clingwrap. The mayonnaise flicked across his knees as he unstuck the clingy layers.

This was Monday.

'I know Donna emailed around last term, which seems like ages ago, but I've been trying to say hello to everyone in person,' a woman said as she sat down next to Bryce. 'Sorry I didn't manage it before now.'

Bryce looked up from his mangled sandwich and was startled by two things in succession. One, she looked like his wife: same rosy glowing hair the same length, same hazel eyes that crinkled the same way with smiling, same oval-shaped face. Two, she looked unlike his wife: wingnut ears, chin more pointed and prominent, long fringe cut square at the brow line.

A paralysing thought struck Bryce—that Death had reconfigured her and now she was returned but changed. Perhaps Death had conjured her as an anniversary gift. Bryce did not want this gift from Death.

Don't look, he told himself, staring back at the food in his hands—think of the differences.

'I'm Fiona,' she said, and held out a hand, then withdrew it when he showed her the mayonnaise on his fingers.

'Bryce,' he said. 'Science.'

'I'm Music and Maths.'

There, another difference. Bryce straightened up, felt air leak into his lungs. June had been a botanist, advising on policy in the government's conservation department. She was a fine statistician, but it was the plants she loved, not how their populations might be numerically modelled. As for music, she had preferred silence, though if the occasion called for it, she usually opted for the simple pleasures of Seventies disco.

'Sounds like a rare thing,' he said. 'A double degree?'

'Double major. Maths can be taught within a BA. Any dual duties for you?'

Bryce was still eyeballing his lunch. 'Chemistry. Primary burden is Biology. I did a master's in Biochemistry.' He lifted the sandwich to his mouth and took a bite.

'Sounds very Jekyll and Hyde.'

He grinned briefly, feeling the clumps of bread around his teeth. June hadn't disliked literature, but neither had she seen the point of it beyond idle entertainment. Her bookish interests were in esoteric texts and illuminated manuscripts. She'd hunt them out in libraries and museums wherever they travelled on holiday. Though her favourite book, as she liked to declare after a few glasses of syrah, was a venerable classic—a work of true poetry, drawing upon a language deeper than language itself: the *Yates Garden Guide*.

'Mm. Arguably we can all be—reduced to chemistry,' Bryce said. 'Including our moral impulses.'

'It was a pretty downbeat story.' Fiona tapped a corner of the *New Zealand Geographic* on Bryce's lap, her knuckles scraping the hem of his shorts. Bryce's leg gave a little jump. 'Is that good reading?'

She bit into an apple he hadn't noticed she was holding.

'I browse it—cover to cover,' he said, and thought, The dead don't eat. Eating is surely reserved for the living.

He could hear the machinery of her mouth working steadily on the food. He searched for a line of questioning to thread through the growing silence, and resisted the creeping

urge to ask if she had any memories of *the time before.* Best
not to indulge supernatural thoughts. Best to keep to what
is real, if for no reason other than some politeness owed to
the living—who eat apples.

Fiona swallowed, said, 'Did you go straight into teaching?'

'I dabbled around after university. Found some orthodox
work in a medical laboratory.' A familiar anecdote, easily
repeated. 'Testing blood and excrement samples, for the
most part. Very process-driven. After two years, I began to
wonder if a more dynamic profession might be preferable.'

'When was that?'

'Twenty-five years ago.'

'Quite some time. You must enjoy it'—she gestured
with the apple, holding it out as if offering it to him—'the
teaching business.'

He peered at her, and she flashed him a smile. Teeth like
June's—small white stones, incisors squared-off and level
with the rest.

'It's more or less become another process,' he said. 'I
teach certain known solutions to certain known problems.'

'Science isn't more creative than that?'

'In high school? No. Perhaps you're thinking of geniuses
like Charles Darwin, Rosalind Franklin, Louis Pasteur. Or
the lofty alchemists pursuing the philosopher's stone?'

'I just thought "leaps of imagination" was a sort of
scientific ethos.'

'No doubt it is,' he said. 'You're new to teaching?'

'Professionally, yes. I taught piano informally, in the
evenings, when I was working at the nursery.'

'Nursery?'

'Sure. Growing plants for garden centres around the
country.'

Fiona bit once more into the apple.

Bryce crammed the remainder of his sandwich into his mouth.

June had worked for the government her whole career. Briefings and budget bids and endless bloody meetings, she'd said. But all very keen and green, as far as possible, within the constraints. At home, she had spent every hour she could in the garden. Perhaps she had bedded in plants that Fiona had nurtured.

'It was tough, picking up a class late in the year, from a temp,' Fiona said. 'As Donna said, that's the workforce shortage for you. But I feel like I've got good mojo going into this year.'

'It's odd,' Bryce said. 'I can't recall—seeing you around.'

'Different departments, I guess?'

'Mm-hmm.' Bryce squeezed his eyes shut. 'Makes sense.'

'I don't usually hang out in the staffroom—it gets airless. I will, come winter. But this time of year, there's a nice suntrap behind the gym. I'd only thought I might mop up some new faces in here.' She nibbled the edges of her apple core.

Who else could she be yet to meet? It felt like he was last on her list. Why was he last on her list? What had she already garnered about him—what information had other people already furnished her with? It seemed unusual he hadn't met her before now—not impossible, but not likely

Bryce searched for a corroborating strand of reality. 'There's another teacher who works across departments. Relieves in Physics but primarily teaches History. We've talked though I don't often—see him beyond the Science building.'

'Right. Dylan Somebody, yeah?'

'Mm—yes.'

'Are you feeling okay?'

It was true, Bryce was feeling poorly. It was like being buried in sand, the weight of it gradually constricting the body and breath before the grains finally trickle past the lips, down the throat.

'It's been—nice—meeting you,' he spluttered.

He stood up, clutching his clingwrap and his magazine, the mug of cold tea forgotten under his seat. He headed for the door, skirting around the tables, and nearly collided with Jackson and Gilroy, likewise on their way out. Gilroy glowered as Bryce bustled past, but Jackson offered a sympathetic nod, which Bryce, blinkered by his need for escape, did not catch.

Bryce passed the wall of pigeonholes, shouldered the glass swing doors and strode halfway across the overbridge that connected the staff area with the forecourt outside the administration block. There was some glare, but Bryce didn't think Donna was at her window. He felt the warm sick fill his mouth and he leaned over the railing. A small group of boys were gathered below, like trolls lurking in the bridge's shadow.

'Sir,' one of them said, bowing deeply.

'Keeping out of trouble?' said another.

Bryce swallowed.

'Don't take the mick,' he barked. Standing up straight, he finished crossing the overbridge to the forecourt, looked across and saw Donna at the window and waved to her, telling himself, You are a basically sound and stable man, Bryce. The dead are not truly risen, and the world is not ending.

He discarded his clingwrap in a flip-top wheelie bin, which the caretaker was busy filling with fistfuls of chip packets and soft-drink cans and paper bags and fruit peelings and all the rest of the lunchtime detritus.

Heading along the winding, downhill path towards the Science block, Bryce forced himself to conceive of another difference. He found one: she looked like his wife not as he'd last known her, but as she'd looked when she was about thirty-five, fifteen years before Death stalked her through the wilderness.

This realisation helped Bryce not at all.

The night was black and the lake was black. He waded into the heavy water. He had an expectation, like a memory, that the surface of the lake should be blank, but it was pricked with stars. He almost could have navigated by them if their patterns weren't so unfamiliar. His wife was there, around him, but he did not reach for any part of her. He kept walking, the drag increasing as his body became more submerged. Up to his chest, his neck, his chin. Up to his lips, his nose. He closed his eyes and went under. He stood on the rocky bottom, bounded entirely by the water, feeling its closeness around him, its constant, gentle pressure. The unseen depths beyond. Something wrapped softly around him—a pair of long and bloodless arms. He reached out to meet the embrace and the water pushed against him, resisting. A scream came through the water, distant at first then filling his ears. The water caught at his arms as he struggled up and out of sleep, tangled in his sheets.

There came another scream in the night, from the world outside, and he knew it as the screeching of the possums in the trees.

It had been a summer of nightmares, this first long summer without June. He worked himself free of the bedding, and rose and made a mug of strong, sweet coffee. Facing east, sitting on their old sofa amongst the curtains of foliage drooping from the pots that dominated the living room—as others did the study, and others the guest room, and others the porch—he listened to the layered noises of the night and waited for the sun.

At lunch on Tuesday, nobody was in his corner. He made his way towards the cluster of empty seats. Halfway across the room, she called his name. The world fell away and he froze, poised beyond the boundary of the known universe. Then he felt his trajectory adjust. He sat down beside her and placed his mug of tea and copy of *New Zealand Geographic* under his chair.

'Hello,' he said.

'Howdy.' Death's gift, smiling graciously. 'How're you, Bryce?'

He noticed a pinch of reticence in her voice. She was concerned, but cautious.

'Sorry for running off yesterday,' he said, not looking at her, thinking, Wingnut ears, wingnut ears, wingnut ears.

'It was a little sudden. I enjoyed chatting. You sure you're okay?'

'Yes, thank you.' Bryce forced out a chuckle, which sounded like choking. 'All these years of teaching, and I still get nervous on the first day of school.'

'I did wonder if the nerves ever disappear,' she said, and snapped open an old takeaway container. Penne with a plain tomato sauce. 'At least we're all in the same boat.'

'I suppose we are,' Bryce said, and thought, Though no two of us is kept awake at night by exactly the same thing.

'Fair point,' Fiona replied. 'Mind if I ask what's keeping

you up at night?'

A dislocating shock—the inner voice transgressing, becoming outer voice.

'Gardening,' Bryce whispered.

'Gardening?'

'Can't keep on top of it.'

'It gets the better of a lot of people.'

Bryce hastily peeled the clingwrap from his lunch and took a bite. Today's sandwich was in better condition. He had been careful to place it on top of the objects in his shoulder bag that could cause it real damage, and which had caused yesterday's sandwich so much damage. The main offender was a hefty Biology textbook he'd pilfered from the department's expired stock two years ago. The book's major appeal was its hand-drawn illustrations. They resembled those of the books Bryce had been taught from in the Seventies—it may have been the same artist—which displayed a creative bravura lacking in the slick photos and anaemic CAD drawings of the modern textbooks. June had likewise admired the illustrations—the botanical sketches especially, and the charming little animals.

'I hope nobody's been causing you trouble enough,' Bryce said, 'to keep you awake at night?'

'Most of the boys seem well-behaved,' Fiona said. 'Fairly good engagement across the years. No real trouble I can't handle.'

'A professional summary,' Bryce said. 'I hear you're doing great.'

No real trouble, but trouble nonetheless.

Fiona lifted penne from the container to her lips. 'Ear to the grapevine, eh?' She put the penne into her mouth.

'I don't mean to suggest gossip.'

'People will always say things to keep themselves entertained.'

He bit off more of his sandwich, chewed quickly, bit off more again. In parallel, she forked penne from the container, finishing it off.

He balled up his clingwrap and squeezed it, released it, squeezed it. 'Is any particular boy giving you trouble?'

'How do you mean?'

'You said you're having not much trouble—but some?'

He rolled the ball of clingwrap between his palms, a residue of mayonnaise and tomato juice coating his skin.

She laughed. 'It's nothing, honestly. Last year I had this class clown, a boy called Benny, in my Year 10 Maths class and—lo and behold!—this year he's in my Year 11 Maths class. He's just an attention-seeker. Or else, who knows, maybe it's misdirected adolescent affection. That's the age group, I suppose. Under-developed brains and an over-supply of hormones.'

'I recognise the name.'

'Excuse me, Bryce?' Jackson had snuck up on them. He squatted down next to Bryce, resting easily on his haunches. 'Glad I caught you. That circulatory model of yours—do you mind if I borrow it again?' He added as an aside to Fiona, 'It has this rubber tubing on hooks, and a foot pump. Kids love to see the red dye sploshing around, especially if a bit spills out.'

'When—do you need it?'

'Is tomorrow morning okay?'

'I'll dig it out,' Bryce said, unsure of where exactly he'd need to dig. Over the holidays, some well-meaning person had tidied the Science department's supply room. He should have told Jackson that the ancient, leaky contraption had finally been consigned to the bin—it might be true.

'Champion,' Jackson said, and he clasped Bryce's arm.

Bryce remembered it was this time last year that Aidan Jackson had hugged him in the supply room.

The resumption of school, after the summer June went missing, had promised the return of structure and purpose to Bryce's days. But while that promise had been fulfilled, and the days were easier, routines may only reorganise reality, not replace it. In quiet moments, Bryce had felt his grief pushing against the inside of his skin. Then one day, hunting amongst the shelves of equipment, searching for the razor kits—in his next class, they would be preparing thin leaf sections to inspect the cells under microscopes—Bryce had begun to shiver. He was crying when Jackson stumbled into the room with an elbow pressing down the lever handle and a foot pinning open the door, arms loaded up with the circulatory model he was seeking to return. The two men had stared at each other in shock. Bryce registered some dismay as Jackson roughly deposited the model on the floor. The larger, younger Physical Education teacher had then grabbed Bryce and—his nose flattened against a firm pectoral muscle, the muskiness of the neighbouring armpit an unexpected comfort—Bryce had wept for several minutes.

He'd preferred that it was Jackson who found him in the supply room, and not one of his immediate colleagues. There was solace and safety offered in the moment, but afterwards no expectations' or awkwardness. The men remained independent of each other.

Jackson had, however, come to June's wake. The *fake wake*. That was June's brother's clumsy joke. The police had been clear in setting everybody's expectations. No one lost

hope entirely, but as more time elapsed, other possibilities
gained better odds. There wasn't much to go on, said the
police. There had been June's car near the entrance to the
hiking trail, and there had been two or three possible early
sightings, and there had been some evidence of a camp site.
Then there had been nothing, and no body. After four slow,
painful months passed, his brother-in-law encouraged Bryce
to hold a small ceremony—not the real deal, of course, more
of a . . . *oh dear!*—to help everybody along in the process
of mourning. Were they mourning, if nothing had been
confirmed? Some form of healing, they agreed, was required.

Naturally, a fake wake suggested the same thing as the real
deal. And just as naturally, the absence of a body raised a few
questions and a few eyebrows. Bryce's desire for privacy was
interpreted by some in June's family as a need for secrecy. He
had always been a head-scratcher for them, being the quiet
sort, whereas June was considered more outgoing. But they
were both quiet people, Bryce knew. June was simply better
at hiding her preference for solitude. In the end, even fewer
members of June's family attended the wake than Bryce
had anticipated. Bryce's two sisters and brother—gathered
together in one room for the first time since their father died,
a year after their mother—at first gave their condolences
then, drinking steadily, proposed several upsetting reasons
for optimism. From school, the Head of Science and several
colleagues attended. And then there was Jackson, who came
alone and made his excuses politely but promptly as soon as
the speeches were concluded, as did most of the other guests.

'You're a real lifesaver, Bryce,' Jackson said presently,
pushing up from his squat to a standing position without
apparent effort.

'A *champion* lifesaver,' Fiona said.

Jackson winced.

'What?' Fiona said. 'Your words.'

'Nothing. All good.' Jackson glanced at Bryce. 'I should prep for class. Nice to see you again, Fiona. And you, Bryce.'

'Sure. Catch you around, Aidan,' Fiona said.

Bryce said nothing.

Jackson gave them two thumbs up then bounded away, collecting an acerbic-looking Gilroy near the door.

Fiona turned back to Bryce. 'I better shoot as well. If you ever need tips on managing your garden, let me know.'

Bryce gaped at her.

She tapped her temple. 'I worked in logistics at the nursery. A lot of planning goes into keeping living things alive, fresh for sale, with as few casualties as possible. Though we'd compost any plants that didn't survive. "Waste not, want rot" was the motto, or one of the many mottos.'

'Want rot,' Bryce said, breathless.

'Nature is a great recycler, as you must be well aware,' Fiona said, and she winked and clucked her tongue.

The skies were clearing but the markings of a storm were everywhere in the sodden, sparkling bush. Immersed beneath the water, he was being propelled across the lake's immense diameter. Pushed by the long slosh of the seiche. Her limbs enfolded him, comforting him, keeping him under. He wasn't aware of holding his breath though he must have been, and for how long? His vision turned milky, the water transforming into a thick white fog. Then he couldn't breathe at all. He woke up gasping, a soreness encircling his neck as if he had just been throttled.

A tin shed was nestled in the overgrown, evergreen garden at the rear of the house. Lopsided and rusted in spots, the shed was nevertheless weathertight and neatly stacked with decades' worth of this and that. In the light of the torch that he held in his mouth, he slid out an offcut of plywood from along one wall. He lugged it around to the front porch, where a steady amber glow spilled through the open doorway from the hall. He returned to the shed to collect a pot of dark green paint, a small brush, four nails and a hammer. On the plywood he painted in large, neat capitals: PRIVATE SALE ENQUIRE WITHIN. He deliberated about adding a phone number, and decided against it for the moment. First, he would purchase a cheap mobile phone for the purpose.

He tore out the estate agent's staple with the claw of the hammer, and before the paint had finished drying on the new sign, he nailed it to the railing.

Wednesday, the nadir of the week, and Bryce already felt exhausted. He traversed the final stage of his assigned quadrant for lunchtime patrol. It covered the Science block, around to the Art block, then down through a grimy industrial region overlooked by the staffroom, and lastly past the gym. The route, Bryce had noted with relief when he inspected the schedule on the whiteboard in the staff kitchenette, passed nowhere in sight of the Music or Maths buildings.

Approaching the gym, he noticed that the walls of poured concrete—which marked the industrial region, a space that was the caretaker's domain—seemed to have become more pitted and stained, more wickedly defaced. The expanse of asphalt more cracked and weedy. A stench hung in the air as though the caretaker had spent the summer trapping possums—Bryce had heard them screaming here too, on late nights, in the pine trees along the school's boundary—

and stored their carcasses in the big skips for the duration of those hot, sticky months.

Most of the school was like this. The place was starved of funding. A five-year property refresh plan had stretched into a ten-year plan, and was now, Bryce understood, in the region of twenty-plus years, with a regular re-stacking of priorities. Money had been injected into the construction of a new Science block the year before last, due only to mounting concerns about the safety of the previous building. *Complaints* was really the word. The *concerns* had gone ignored until three classrooms of boys and their teachers were poisoned by a gas leak and ended up painting the benches and floors, then the pavement outside, with the sickly contents of their stomachs. Systemic issues were swiftly uncovered. The Board was placed under statutory management, and a new Principal was urgently sought. Cash was meanwhile redirected, and designs for a high-spec, non-life-threatening Science block were drawn up. New to the hot seat, Donna fought to gain the trust of the government busybodies—and the community of incensed parents—and drag the school's reputation out of the ditch. The reality was, however, that even before the accidental poisoning of eighty-seven people, the school was not, and never would be, high on anybody's list to attend—neither to learn nor to teach. Where one wound up was largely a matter of where one happened to reside, in the former case, or where the jobs happened to be, in the latter. Luck and circumstance are geographical factors, Bryce reflected. We exist at the mercy of our environments—which we insist on degrading to the fullest extent possible.

And yet here was a pleasant warmth radiating down on the top of his head, and a brightness filling his eyes despite the surrounding palette of greys. There was a bench seat, and Bryce considered having a rest in the sunshine before the bell went.

'You found my little suntrap,' Fiona said.

She came at him from a corner darkened by a conflation of shadows, where two other people were huddled—Jackson and Gilroy.

'We've just been having a confab.' Fiona tipped her head towards the shadows. In her hand she held the remains of a jammy bagel. 'De-stressing, really.'

She pecked at the bagel. Quite a change from yesterday's penne. Red bits around the mouth, still.

'Nice looking lunch,' Bryce said, and he thought of the sandwich he had eaten earlier, while still on patrol. The same salad filling between the same wholewheat bread as the day before, the same as the day before that—and all the preceding years before that. Learn to live a little, June had once said, slathering chilli jam on a slice of bread and passing it to him. After she'd left for work, he'd wiped the chilli jam off, fed the bread to the birds, then replaced the top slice on his sandwich. Returning home after school, he noticed fat blobs of excrement all over the porch steps. Something's sure got into the birds today, June complained when she came in the door a short time later, removing her cardigan to dab at the soiled shoulder with a damp towel.

'Cream cheese and jam. Good comfort food, though I hardly planned that to be the case. Heck. My problems are nothing compared to theirs.' Fiona indicated the shadows again. 'I just need to figure that Benny out.'

'Have you heard?' Jackson said, moving quickly to stand at Bryce's elbow. Bryce could see the distress on his face.

'No,' Bryce said. 'I'm guessing I haven't.'

'Perrin, the bastard,' Jackson said.

'He's threatening to go to Donna,' Fiona said.

Gilroy hissed at Fiona.

'Bryce is friendly,' Jackson said, but Gilroy looked at Bryce with disgust.

Jackson sighed and threw up his hands. 'It will be all over the school soon enough.'

'Ron caught—you know Ron Perrin, from Economics?' Fiona said.

Bryce nodded.

'He caught these lovebirds'—and here she smiled, kindly, reassuringly, first at Jackson then at Gilroy—'having a snog in the gym's back office.'

'He's going to blackmail us,' Gilroy said, edging out from the shadows.

'For what, though?' Fiona said. 'I mean, really! He's a peeping Tom, I say. A peeping Ron!'

Gilroy grabbed Jackson by the arm and dragged him away several steps. 'I don't trust the black widower,' he whispered, loud enough, deliberately enough.

'We'll be finito soon anyway,' Jackson said plainly.

'My lips are sealed,' Bryce said, and he turned away from them all.

'Bryce?' Fiona said.

'I need to make a cup of tea,' Bryce said. Then, 'Incoming.'

Jackson and Gilroy stood apart at the sound of the approaching students.

'I'll come with you,' Fiona said. She called over her shoulder, 'We'll catch up later. Don't sweat anything just yet.'

'I had no idea,' Bryce said, and began reviewing what he knew about Jackson and Gilroy, the scraps that might reveal the meal.

'I had some idea.' Fiona popped the last of the bagel into her mouth.

They walked in silence up to the forecourt by the administration block.

Crossing the overbridge together, Fiona said, 'I didn't like what James called you back there. I don't need to know the story—though I'm all ears if you ever want to talk. Aidan mentioned you lost your wife, but I don't know anything really. It just wasn't a nice thing for James to say.'

Black widower.

Bryce had never heard the term applied to him before— hadn't known it ever had been applied to him—and his insides churned that this was the name by which the other staff knew him. June's family must have used similar words. As if it were him, hiding in the foliage, springing forth on quick legs, out in the depths of the bush. They really ought to ask Death what happened, for only He was sure to know.

Fiona got ahead of him and stopped, then Bryce stopped, and she turned to face him.

'I wish them both well, but James can be a real jerk,' she said. 'I'm sure Aidan could get with someone far nicer.'

'He's truly—some type—I suppose—of charismatic megafauna.'

Fiona screwed up her face. 'You mean, like a large attractive animal?'

Bryce moved his head in a small figure-of-eight, a nod and a shake at the same time.

'You mean, unlike *un*charismatic *minor*-fauna?'

'It's a comment—June used to make—' and he felt his wife jab him in the ribs as celebrities prowled the length of the red carpet on television: There's a fine-looking herd of charismatic megafauna. Untouchable cash magnets. No more essential than the rest of us, except nobody's lining up to throw bundles of money at you and me every time we smile nicely.

'Sorry—your wife?'

And she'd tickle him under his chin, behind his ears, between his thighs, and say, You give me a nice smile and I'll give you anything you like.

'I'm not sure—I don't know exactly—what I meant.'

Fiona nodded. 'Sometimes, inside my head, it's like a kaleidoscope.'

Bryce made for the glass swing doors, sweat prickling his skin. Fiona followed him through, then into the kitchenette.

He rummaged around in an overhead cabinet, looking for a clean mug, making a fuss of the job, keeping Fiona blocked from view behind the cabinet door.

'I'm going to get murdered tomorrow,' June's voice said. 'But I wonder if I can just avoid that?'

Bryce gripped the shelf to steady himself.

'I can't stand getting murdy.'

'I didn't murder anyone,' Bryce rasped.

'Oh—of course not!' Fiona said. 'James is, frankly, a bully. I can't believe he said what he said.'

Bryce pushed several mugs around, clinking them against each other. 'You said that you're—going— to get—'

'I'm absolutely bound to get muddied,' Fiona said, then gave a shocked laugh. '*Muddied*! Not *murdered*!' She tapped the whiteboard showing the lunchtime patrol schedule. 'I'm listed for the sports field tomorrow, and it's meant to pour down all morning. Hopefully it rains through until home time, and they just play a movie in the hall or something at lunch break.'

Bryce placed a mug on the Formica bench, and Fiona reached across to click the cabinet door shut. He turned his back and began an overlong struggle with the air-locked container of tea bags. Scrambling to change the subject, he said, 'Did you feel—as though sometimes you were heading—in two directions at once—studying Music and Mathematics?'

She paused, and he inspected the tea bags, selecting one from beneath the top layer. He shook it over the sink, checking for tears. Fiona was leaning against the wall beside the patrol schedule, gazing at the tea-towel cubby opposite.

'They're both things I enjoy,' she said. 'To me, Music is a form of felt Mathematics. It sounds mad, and people usually scoff when I say this—'

Bryce dropped the tea bag into the mug, and realised that she'd fallen silent. Her head was turned towards him.

'I won't scoff,' he said.

She smiled, and faced the cubby again. 'Mathematical notations often seem to me like musical ones—and vice versa. I feel them in my body. If I'm grappling with a difficult equation or a complex section of a score, I find that if I relax my body into it, the solution usually surfaces. I don't know how it works, but it does.'

'The mind—is an emergent phenomenon,' he said, and saw that his hand—fingers hooked through the handle of the mug, poised beneath the tap of the boiler—that his hand was shaking. 'It arises from—processes in the body. Throughout the animal classes, different orders of mind exist. Though subjective consciousness—self-consciousness—is another leap again.'

He depressed the lever and scalding water dribbled into the mug.

'At what point do dreams come into the mix?' Fiona said. 'I can just imagine an octopus thrashing its tentacles around during some awful nightmare in its bedroom. What scares an octopus—sharks? I *hate* sharks. Every night, me and poor Occy could be waking up, scared to death by the same terrible visions. Don't let us watch any re-runs of *Jaws* before bedtime. Ouch! Let me get the cold tap.'

'It's only a splash,' Bryce said, setting down the overflowing mug. He placed his hand under the cool water.

Fiona handed him a tea towel to dry his hands, and her fingertips found his as he accepted it from her.

'Thank you,' he said, and looked up and was blinded. The glass doors, and the world beyond them, were lost to a liquid white light spilling around her, or from her. Bright though the light was, her features were plain to see, and he saw that June was smiling, her face framed by her long hair, dripping aflame from her crown down to her chest. An angel, and still my protector, Bryce thought. Then a darkness entered her face, and a thought wormed into his brain: I relied too much on you. And in my reliance I became pitiful, and knowing this I became embittered and—shamefully—at times vicious. You saw it was always in me. The worm dug in, and Bryce knew: I am that way still, though with no one to rely upon, and therefore only more pitiful.

The sun winked out behind a cloud and June vanished, leaving Fiona in her place. An instant later the bell rang, shaking the world as violently as a bomb blast, and Bryce felt for a moment as if he might be ripped apart.

'Half the week down, another half to go,' Fiona said after the noise stopped, and she wriggled a finger around in her ear to clear the buzzing.

Stepping out of the kitchenette, they joined the flow of teachers exiting the staffroom, a rush of bodies across the overbridge, his abandoned mug of tea a distant memory.

A woman dressed all in black and grey, the Head of Music Studies, whose name Bryce could not remember, touched Fiona's shoulder and offered to accompany her to her next class. Still twisting the tea towel in his hands, Bryce moved across the forecourt in the opposite direction, cutting through the crowds of chattering students towards the Science block, a great heaviness within him shifting.

At last period, one amongst the twenty-six juniors decided to draw a large, flaccid penis on the whiteboard and, beside it, a pair of elongated parentheses containing a set of uncertain squiggles. Bryce had been out back collecting a bin of Bunsen burners, which he'd struggled to locate, when the drawing was hastily done.

'What is this?' he asked, looking at the whiteboard as he set the clunking bin down on the front workbench.

'We hoped you'd know the answer, sir,' said Benny, outing himself, already red-faced with derring-do.

'Why do you say that?'

'It's on *your* whiteboard, sir,' Benny said, puffing himself up. 'So *you* must know something about it.'

Bryce watched the boy with a steady gaze. His theory—bolstered by an impatience that was the shadow of his increasing exhaustion—was that you really needed to nip them in the bud, especially the imps like Benny, and you couldn't do it too soon. This was something every teacher eventually learned, even those who were instinctively generous and agreeable, like Fiona—though they inevitably took the long way to learning it and suffered far more as a consequence.

Benny's face took on a bilious sheen.

'Common property, these whiteboards,' Bryce said. 'Whoever makes use of them takes the lesson. Why don't you get us started, Benny. Stand up and come to the front. Don't keep us waiting. Come right to the front and explain what we are seeing here. Come along. I can see that everybody's very eager to hear what you have to say. Your peers are possessed with a great thirst for knowledge. That's right. Now stand up straight. Have a little confidence. Truly, the picture on the left speaks of great confidence, though perhaps it's merely an overcompensation. I don't suppose it matters much, judging by the picture on the right. You may need to spend a bit more time explaining that one, because I'm not sure the artist has depicted the real thing very well. Perhaps their powers of observation have been hindered by a lack of any actual observations. Begin, Benny. Don't be shy. Get going, or you'll see a month of detention.'

He washed up on the farthest shore. Raising his head, he saw the lake before him, as broad and flat as always. He rested his head back down, on a flat rock still warm from the sun, and lay slowly drying in the evening air. The edge of the forest canopy was silhouetted like a decal on the cerulean dome. He listened to the sound of the cooling air settling upon the forest's many surfaces as darkness wove itself into the scene. The full silver moon slid into view and he lay beneath it for the equivalent of many nights before its sister filled the world again with golden light. He could no longer recall his purpose, and so he lay in the warm rays, hearing like the rocks. He tried to picture his home, and could not. This unsettled him, and he tried to lift himself up. But a coldness gripped his ankles, and with a terrible swiftness, he was being dragged across the stones. *You have murdy me,* a voice said, and although it sounded utterly unlike her, he knew it to be his wife's. My wife, who I came here to find, and who I found, and who I forgot, and who I have done nothing to save. These were his thoughts as his body was taken once more into the lake, as that altered voice repeated its accusation: *You have murdy me. You have murdy me. You have murdy me.*

The paint had dripped where it was thickest—from the terminal points of the letters. He looked down at the paper in his hand, at the sums it contained, and dropped another thirty thousand off the end. He dipped the paint brush into the can and put the figure at the bottom of the sign, with the letters ONO in the lower right corner. He returned the can and brush to the shed and took out a low wooden platform on wheels with a long rope handle. He would begin with the plants on the porch, at first only sorting and shifting, before de-cluttering in earnest once it became necessary to consider such things.

The rain began and ended within an hour on Thursday morning, staining the air with a fresh, earthy smell that Bryce enjoyed. Before lunch he was free of classes—an 'administrative duties' period. He marked a stack of Genetics papers beside the tiny garden where the Horticulture students laboured over their projects. Checking his pigeonhole near the end of the period, he discovered a crisp note folded into quarters. Written in elegant, looping cursive across the neat black lines of a fresh music sheet:

> *Coffee sometime, off school grounds?*
> *—F♯*

The loose, free handwriting was entirely different from the cramped style of his wife's. Yet he gasped—a strangled, scraping sound. He screwed up the note, dropped it into the kitchenette bin and went outside, crossing the overbridge down its centre, afraid if he ventured too near the sides his shuddering body would tip over the edge.

Five minutes later he strode back across the overbridge and plucked the note out of the bin. He smoothed it out on the bench and looked at its dampened and stained surface, at the words penned so perfectly, and wondered at his anger, at the shock still reverberating through him.

'How's the world of natural wonders?' Jackson asked, clapping him on the back, and he yelped and screwed up the note again.

'You're a jumpy one, Bryce,' Jackson said.

'Everything is fine.'

'I heard you gave Benny a good fright yesterday afternoon,' Jackson said, and snorted. 'He's a little devil, that one. I just saw him leaving Donna's office with his parents. Cat's bum looks on their faces. They've put Donna in a mood. I was nervous already when she called me in, as you are in a special position to appreciate. Turned out she wanted to discuss a request I made roughly half a year ago.' Jackson rubbed his thumb and fingers together: moolah. 'You think it's too much to ask for a new set of basketballs every so often? Every other week, we have to pump the old ones back up. But do you know what Donna said? She said pumping basketballs sounded good for my biceps, so I should consider it professional development. Even the Principal thinks that PE teachers are just apes. Shocker. You know, I was teaching a class today about the effects of exercise on the cardiovascular system, and its positive impacts on mental health? We also discussed how exercise helps develop neurons in the hippocampus. That was just one class.'

Bryce blinked.

'Sorry, Bryce. I'm feeling a bit all over the show.' Jackson sighed. 'Bugger the basketballs, so long as she's not calling me in for a more *personal* conversation. Anyway. Benny and his parents have slinked away now. Slunk? I think Donna wants to see you. By that I mean, she asked me to send you to see her. Sorry. We saw you running around like a headless chook out there.'

Bryce's fingernails were cutting into his palms, deeper and deeper. He could feel the note dissolving in the pit of his fist.

'Just sometime today, Donna said. I'm sorry about it, Bryce.'

'Right.'

'Are you good, Bryce?' Jackson placed his two enormous hands upon Bryce's shoulders. 'We need to really look after each other in this world. We must work to be happy in ourselves, and we must help others to be happy in themselves also. The year has only just begun! We should grab a beer together sometime.'

Jackson released Bryce's shoulders.

'Right.' Bryce went through the doors to the overbridge, Jackson at his side. 'I don't actually drink, these days.'

'I think that would be good,' Jackson said. 'I'm going to say straight up that I worry about you sometimes, Bryce. I think about you, and I worry about you.'

'Aidan, I wouldn't ever say anything—'

'You're a reliable guy. Oh, hey—the circulatory model worked a treat, again. You're a bona fide genius. I have one more class to demo it with, then it will be back safe and sound with you. I ought to tell you that I did patch up a couple of joins, just following an instance where a jet of fluid shot across the front row. But the kids all—mostly—laughed their socks off. I'd better leave you to take that call.'

Bryce hadn't recognised the ringing as coming from within his personal sphere, from the pocket of his own shorts. He fished out the phone and thumbed the answer button.

A stranger coughed, then said, 'Hi, I hope this isn't a bad time . . . I'm calling about the private sale?'

Bryce fixed his eyes on the miniature beagle, the size of a fist, mounted near the edge of the desk. Its plastic head was connected to a plastic spring, which disappeared into a void inside the plastic collar. Its large, painted eyes were imploring, and a needful grin with human teeth stretched across its face.

Bryce suspected that Donna thought of it as a 'colourful touch' in the otherwise starkly professional office.

Was it important that the beagle also seemed to suggest Donna as a sniffer-out of facts—even of truths? Did it really matter what Benny had conveyed to his parents, and what they in turn had conveyed to Donna?

'It represents a rather shocking lack of maturity on your part.'

'Thank you, Donna.'

'For what exactly, Bryce?'

'For your magnanimity.'

'We will need to issue a written apology, on school letterhead. I will author it, and you will co-sign.'

'Did Benny's parents make any demands?'

'None that I'm prepared to meet in real terms. Not yet, at least.'

'My head on a stick, perhaps?'

'For now, I will be satisfied with a drop of your blood to ink the signatures.'

Bryce lifted his eyes to meet Donna's, and expressed his consent with a series of rapid blinks.

'Good chat with Aidan Jackson? He seemed to find you quite promptly. He's been hounding me for a bigger budget since his promotion to Head of Health and Phys Ed. I presume he was griping to you. He needn't worry. He'll get his basketballs in time for mid-winter Christmas. Your conversation seemed, from what I could see, rather energetic. No angst worth sharing?'

'Not to my knowledge.'

'You sound evasive, Bryce.'

'I'm not.'

'Just checking. Well.' Donna clapped her hands once and examined her desk calendar. 'There's a group of us that go to spin classes every Thursday night. The new woman in Mathematics and Music—Fiona Sharp—suggested the idea last year. You've been introduced to Fiona? Ten of us, a mix of men and women, have been going. It's good for keeping up fitness but also, to be quite honest, it helps clear the head and exorcise some stress.'

Bryce hesitated. 'I prefer walks.'

'I'm not the only older person who goes either, Bryce. It's a good workout but it's not overly hard on the body.' She let a moment pass. 'I'm afraid I need to prepare some papers for the Board now, if you wouldn't mind shutting the door on the way out, please.'

Bryce left Donna's office and made his way to the staffroom.

He would have screamed until his larynx shredded if some ghoul or goon had disturbed his lunch.

But Bryce was permitted by chance to ingest his sandwich and tea, and browse *New Zealand Geographic*, in his corner, unmolested by any other being. Even Jackson and Gilroy were nowhere to be seen—clearly keeping their heads down. By the end of lunch, he had perused half a dozen articles and prepared a small speech for the caller who'd wanted to look at his house that evening. When the time was up, as he was leaving the staffroom, a recollection thrilled him. That irksome imp Benny wasn't on any of the afternoon's class attendance lists, just as he hadn't been on any that morning. Whatever else Thursdays may end up being—today had already been a manic mess—they would, at the very least, be Benny-free for the rest of the year.

Brambles and the first of the stones scattered in the undergrowth. Snares of supplejack catching at his arms, stretching then letting go, pinging back into the bush. The rocky shore and, suddenly, close to his exposed feet: the edge of the lake. In the dusk light, the lake's surface and the sky reflected the same deep vermillion. A rotten feeling of anticipation persisted, but what was he waiting for? The lake sat before him like a dreadful promise. A twig snapped and he turned to find a boy, thirteen or fourteen years old, wearing the uniform of the school where he taught. A four-colour emblem was stitched onto the grey shirt—chevrons of black, white, yellow, red. 'Excuse us, sir,' the boy said. More of them emerged out of the shadows of the bush, their faces solemn, their hands held behind their backs. There were too many of them, and they were all the same boy. They were all that one boy, Benny. 'Sir,' said the first of the Bennys, 'have you lost something?' Keeping one hand concealed, he brought his other hand around to the front, and in it, gripped by a fistful of copper hair, was her smiling head. The other boys likewise held out a hand, each of them revealing a different part of her. He trembled as the voices of the Bennys washed through him, erasing his borders: 'Sir, have you lost something? Sir, won't you make things right again?'

The uniform of the Bennys in his dream was wrong. The crest of chevrons was new—and yet it was familiar. Troubling also was his sense that the dream reset a timeline. After weeks of the same dream of his wife washing ashore, his dreams this week had moved through a kind of progression. Then tonight, he had been back at the start—fighting the supplejack, cutting his feet on the stones—although that too was different, with the presence of those awful boys in their uniforms.

Still possessed an hour later by the colours of the chevrons, he went out to the shed and, by torchlight, began carefully sorting through box after box, bag after bag. The torch's beam picked out a corner of roughened brown leather. He started tossing things aside, until he uncovered the battered suitcase buried in the back corner. Inside the house, he laid the suitcase beside the coffee table in the living room and cleared the table of its plants and piles of *New Zealand Geographic* magazines. Unlatching the lid of the suitcase, he set aside the old university papers that were heaped on top, then lifted out the large, hardback book and rested it on the table.

It had been an early gift from him to June, a half-joking nod to their sometimes-mystical conversations. It was a replica of a late-seventeenth-century book called *Mutus Liber*—or *Wordless Book*—which illustrated, across fifteen plates, an intricate process of transmutation. The book was not entirely without words. Three of the plates incorporated scraps of Latin, the final being a gesture beyond the book itself, an encouragement to the student who might unlock its peculiar knowledge: *Provided with eyes, thou departest.* Together, he and June had pored over the engraved images.

He stood and retrieved a notepad and pencil, then returned to the table. Tracing his eyes and fingers over the daedal contents of the pages, he took notes on the patterns and themes, sketching out possible interpretations, formulating questions. The trick was to determine exact meanings amidst the apparent ambiguities and contradictions. Though, the book was no more oblique than any number of books filled with rows of precise-seeming text. He'd read works of both prose and poetry that aimed to resist any clear interpretations. This book was not like that. This book merely kept its secrets close. Understood and followed correctly, *Mutus Liber* was a guide through the four foundational stages, often represented by four colours—the same four colours of the chevrons in his dream—towards attainment of the magnum opus.

He felt himself slip backwards through memory, to ideas and conversations from their youth, and he wondered at the capacity of dreams to conjure thoughts long since consigned to the past. *Mutus Liber* was truly a book about many things, but prime amongst them, he saw, it was a book about grief, even a book against grief. It was a book of rejuvenation.

A few hours went by, then he placed the book back inside the suitcase, with his notepad, and put the suitcase away in a closet. Preparing another coffee, he felt as if some small reservoir of energy within him had been tapped into, that he could face the day, the last of this first week, with a degree of self-assuredness that had been absent for too long.

He made a mental note to visit the butcher's before school.

*

He usually reserved the heart for the older boys. A treat
for those students who had elected to study Biology, and
a dramatic flourish to end the first week of the year. It was
a way of showing that, in his own curious way, he could be
magnetic, a man of intrigue. First period of the day, they'd
roared with stunned delight as he revealed the cow's gift
from its wrapper of brown butcher's paper.

'A bloody heart!'

'Bloody is right!'

The older students, astute as always.

But Bryce was unsure if it was forbidden, merely
inappropriate, or perfectly acceptable to expose the younger
ones to such a sight. They were being run through a
mandatory Biology module only, with no expectation of
encountering anything more visceral than a few butchered
sketches on the whiteboard—whether Benny's or his own—
and perhaps a handful of detailed but entirely clinical
diagrams on a worksheet.

In the period right before lunch, the young pack took
their places behind the long rows of benches. He scanned
their faces and spotted no special troublemakers, apart from
Benny at the back, whose smirk made Bryce shiver.

The rest of the class, all slumped shoulders and
weary expressions, looked as if they could do with some
enlivening.

Bryce crossed the room to the rubbish bin by the
entrance. He leaned down and retrieved the package and
returned to the workbench at the front of the class. A few
tugs at a loosened corner and the blotchy brown wrapping
unfolded. Forgetting his gloves, he raised up the meaty heart
with his bare hands.

'This was beating only yesterday, or perhaps the day before,' he said. 'Let me show you how.'

The dissection had of course already occurred. The older students had crowded around while he'd decisively wielded his scalpel, pointing out the heart's major features as, slice by slice, they were revealed: the chambers of the ventricles and atria, the thin flapping valves between them, the aorta. He had poked a gloved thumb into the pulmonary artery to show its astonishing diameter—a cow's heart is anatomically similar to a human's, but much bigger—and the degree of flex that it possessed, engorging and relaxing in rhythm with the beating. This rhythm he had crudely synthesised through the grip and release of his other hand.

Squeezing the great red muscle, he had felt he might reanimate the thing. As though through this simple action, his life force might transfer from his body and into the heart, which would—to be witnessed by everybody present—begin independently pumping again.

He and the class had been filled with awe and verve, and this had buoyed him in a way that further revived his hopes for the day.

That was nearly two hours ago, and Bryce could sense the fumes in his tank dissipating, the threat of emptiness. Part of his psyche had been siphoning off his energy to fuel its own worries—it was the part that knew Fiona would be waiting for him in the staffroom at lunch.

Presently, the heart fell open in several places—the thick tissue still connected at various points—along the lines of incision that he had made earlier. He proceeded to handle the lifeless object badly. It fell from his grip onto the workbench, sending a spattering of red across his shirt. The heart slipped and slopped about, refusing to be grasped, while a wave of titters moved through the class.

'What was it doing in the bin?' a pipsqueak voice asked.

'I hadn't quite intended—on sharing it with you,' Bryce stammered, leaving the heart sitting splayed. He tore several paper towels from the dispenser mounted above the sink. 'I dissected it—for another class—this morning,' he said, patting the heart dry, screwing up the towels as he went. 'But the opportunity to see directly—for yourselves—how a heart works—isn't that too good—to pass up?'

A round of nods, some eager, some not.

'Why let such a good thing—go to waste?'

He held his hands once again above the heart. It might be best, rather than try to manipulate it with his tired, clumsy fingers, to gesture and reveal instead with a pair of tweezers, or tongs.

However—

He was frozen to the spot. The only parts of him capable of motion were his fingers, which trembled. He considered with a strange rationality the opportunity before him. Poised as he was, hands raised dramatically over the heart, he had the full attention of the class. He had only to hope that none of the students would notice the tremors. He had only to hope for that, and to keep his voice calm. A pink blotch flared up on his hand, throbbing precisely where, during that instant of catatonic introspection on Wednesday, he had spilled boiling water on himself. He had to keep calm at the front of this room stuffed full of youthful students, and allow his command of the subject area to facilitate the easy flow of knowledge up from his throat and out of his mouth, while the students sat enraptured and not looking at the tremors, the tremors, the tremors—the uncontrollable tremors of his hands above the lifeless heart—

Which was twitching.

Twitching with a lopsided rhythm.

Twitching with, now, a regular rhythm.

This disembodied and dissected heart, which was indeed pumping independently, was it—

Living?

Non-living?

Dead?

This was a system of categorisation he'd learned to cling to, in moments when simplicity was demanded.

A greenly cascading potted plant: living.

A leaden lump fashioned into a fishing sinker: non-living.

A bee's corpse pinned to a square of polystyrene: dead.

They'd been held up for him, and he'd held them up for others. But the truth of reality was trickier and more slippery. Outside of particular arcana, knowledge tended towards a state of reduction. The pursuit of knowledge was an attempt to render open-ended infinity somehow graspable, manageable, tolerable. Anything but an ineffable nightmare. Yet—dead things may not always stay dead, living things may appear absent of life, and what are we composed of, at our most fundamental levels, if not things which are and always will be non-living?

'Dark stuff, sir.'

'Very grim.'

Another round of nods, and a few hands raised in the air. Then some of the boys leapt to their feet as Bryce's eyes rolled up into his skull and his body fell to the floor. It took one of them half a minute to work up the courage to approach the prone figure of his teacher—who was clutching the cow's dark, wet heart to his chest—behind the workbench. Benny knelt and held a hand over the mouth, unsure if he could feel anything. Careful not to touch the body, he lowered his face and listened for the least sign of breathing.

'Is he alive?' one of the other boys asked, fascinated and afraid.

Benny jumped up and shouted, 'Could one of you idiots please get the Principal!'

The head of the beagle seemed to be quivering so gently that it may not have been quivering at all—only anticipating motion.

Bryce was smiling.

'I understand James Gilroy has advised a possible nervous agitation, leading to fainting, leading to a possible mild concussion, and that he suggests you undergo formal checks. I have called a taxi to take you to the hospital.'

'Thank you, Donna.'

'I'm putting you on a leave of absence.'

'Thank you, Donna.'

'I am also referring you to a wellbeing service. It's voluntary, but I encourage you to take it up. There is a discounted rate. I've made use of it myself in the past and, to be quite honest, it was helpful. There's no obligation to return to work sooner than four weeks from Monday.'

'Thank you, Donna.'

'I will phone around for a substitute over the weekend.'

'That's terrific, Donna.'

'You will of course let us know if we can be of further help? Your health is of genuine importance to me—as it is to your colleagues, and to the Board. We all want the best outcome for you, Bryce.' Donna looked out the window. 'Ah. I see your taxi has arrived. Rest up, Bryce, and stay in touch.'

Bryce rose from the seat. He thrust out an index finger and flicked the beagle's nose sideways, feeling the spring respond with a pliant elasticity. Then, as the beagle's head bobbled at him, Bryce bobbled his head at Donna.

He left the Principal's office still smiling at his apprehension of a miracle. He would ask the taxi driver to take him directly home.

He didn't dream that night, and he didn't go to sleep. He sat amongst the pots on the porch, wrapped in a tartan blanket, consulting *Mutus Liber.* The possums yowled and shrieked in the trees. He thought about Fiona, and about June. Death's gift had been a forgery, but he considered such a thing was not unfeasible. In the undefined hours before dawn, he went out to the shed and took a wooden crate down from a high shelf. From the crate, he removed a small metal leg-trap on a chain. The foot plate rattled in its fitting. A farmer friend had given them the traps when June had grumbled, over drinks at the farmhouse one night, about the possums around their place. The traps came with the offer of a lesson. Taking this up, he had returned to the friend's farm and set traps one Saturday afternoon, stayed the night and shared in some whiskey, then gone back out to collect the animals the following morning. The friend had carried a .22 rifle, explaining it was the most humane way. Though in the city you'll need something quieter, the friend said. Wear gumboots or use something hard and heavy, like a brick, and get to them before any neighbours complain. He'd found himself unable to take the lives of any of the half-dozen possums they found, and the friend had shot each of them once neatly through the head.

There may yet be a justification for killing, he thought. If it means progress can be made, step by step, experimentally, towards a greater goal, ultimately moving in the direction opposite to death, towards life regained—towards the magnum opus, the elixir of *Mutus Liber.*

He returned the trap to the crate, then the crate to the shelf.

Perhaps the killing work was already done. The school's caretaker likely possessed the appropriate skills. Perhaps he should visit after hours, sniff around the skips, see what specimens he might find. If he had no luck, he could approach the caretaker directly. They wouldn't know he had been temporarily absented from the staff roster. Late one quiet afternoon, he would explain to the caretaker, in the mildest terms possible, some convincing basis for his request.

Back in the house, as the coral dawn flooded through the windows, he moved from room to room, watering the hundreds of wilted plants in their pots. He spoke to each one in turn: 'She loved you, did you know? Do you remember very much about her?' He paused for a moment over each plant, head tilted, listening closely, and smiled every so often at the response. 'Ah, yes! Wouldn't it be something special if it was her watering you again. We shall have to be patient, and hope for the best, but prepare for the worst. It has already been a year.'

*
**

Aidan moved through the small living space crowded with the selection of pot plants that Bryce had shifted down from his old place. The living room overlooked an open-air car park. It was a bright and windless Sunday afternoon. Bursts of conversation and laughter and the roar of traffic from the street bounced around to the rear of the building, echoing up through the apartment's narrow louvre windows. Inside the apartment, there was the persistent buzz and rattle of an extractor fan, partially muted behind the bathroom door, which was closed.

Aidan sniffed the air.

'Here we are,' Bryce said, behind him.

Aidan turned and Bryce handed him a mug of tea. Accepting the mug, Aidan confirmed his impression—that Bryce appeared both tired and healthy. There were dark pouches under his eyes, but his eyes were clear and sharp, and his cheeks had a nourished flush.

Bryce sat in one of the two easy-chairs and took a sip of tea.

'Thanks, Bryce,' Aidan said, taking the other chair. 'Cosy place.'

'It suits me, for the time being. Downsizing forced me to undertake some careful sorting.'

'I remember—it was nice, that house you had. Tough after she was gone, I imagine. But this—it's quite handy to town. I got the bus halfway, then decided to walk. Such a beautiful day out. Own or rent?'

'Renting. It's affordable, and the landlord keeps their distance. It's a transitional space. I'll re-settle somewhere else when the time is right.'

'Do what you gotta do.'

'I was fortunate that another teacher from school— Dylan, in History and Physics—he mentioned that this apartment was available. He has one of the places upstairs.'

'Good having someone you already know as a neighbour.'

Bryce smiled around his tea. 'I generally keep to myself.'

'Did—Dylan?—did he tell you about the fiasco at school?'

'Some, not much. We don't see a lot of each other.'

Aidan sniffed again, almost on instinct, and grimaced. He'd sucked in a first shocked breath upon entering the apartment. The smell wasn't overpowering, but it was keenly unpleasant. It was enough that, while Bryce had busied himself making the tea, Aidan had hunted around, amongst the yellowing houseplants, in a cool and explainable, but methodical, manner. He had considered asking to use the bathroom, just as Bryce returned with their two steaming mugs, and then the whole enquiry had felt too intrusive.

Aidan transformed his grimace into a grin.

'I tell you what, that Donna. She's got a heart of gold, beneath that layer of lead, you know. She was very generous to me and James. As generous as she could be.'

'Things worked out all right for you two?'

'Not quite.' Aidan stared into his tea for a moment, then snapped his head back up. 'She gave Ron Perrin the sack. Nothing to do with me and James, mind you. He slapped Benny. Bam! Backhander, right across the cheek.'

'Is that right.'

'There's an investigation. The Board called for it. Looking into the culture of the school.'

'Is that right.'

'Donna found James another job, elsewhere. He transferred six weeks ago. She said the optics of us continuing to teach together were sub-optimal—this was all before the whole fiasco with Ron hitting Benny—but she couldn't ask us to break up. So, she rang in a favour with another friendly principal and soon enough, James went away. After that, I don't really know what happened, Bryce. He stopped returning my calls, and when he finally did answer, he said we were finished, finito.'

'How did Donna learn about you?'

Aidan shrugged. 'It could have been Ron. It could have been kids overhearing a conversation. I guess it was bound to happen. I think they'll let me keep my role as Head of Health and PE.'

'I'm sorry it didn't work out better, Aidan, with you and James.'

'I suppose the grapevine must have gone into overtime, and James saw this as the best way forward for us. I completely disagree. But you know how well scandal mixes with teaching. Donna's a walking case of nervous hives lately. But she's been very supportive. Oh—Fiona says hello.'

'Fiona.'

'She asked that I give you her best wishes.'

'That's kind. Will you tell her that I'm—feeling my way through?'

'Sure. But how *are* you doing, Bryce? How are you holding up?'

'I'm managing all right, really.'

'Yeah?'

'Yes.'

'You contemplating a return to school, or not yet?'

'I haven't decided.' Bryce took a sip then pointed his mug at Aidan. 'Did Donna suggest you pay me a visit?'

Aidan was resting his mug on the exposed skin of his knee. The heat of it was almost too much, but he held the mug there. 'I've been meaning to come say hello, see how you're getting on. But yes, Donna said that, if I was ever to drop by, to let her know how you are.'

'I should have been in more frequent contact. Dylan's mentioned it also. I really have been keeping to myself.'

'It's understandable.'

'It's good to see you, Aidan. It's good to see a friendly face.'

Aidan raised his mug to Bryce, then drank, the tea scalding his throat. He coughed.

'It's nice to be talking with you, Bryce.'

'I recall when you came to June's wake.' Bryce frowned. 'You were the only teacher outside of the handful from Science who attended. Not even Donna came—she sent flowers and an apology card. A double apology. "Sorry for your loss, sorry I can't be there."'

'You had your house done up beautifully. Ribbons on all the plants.' Aidan gazed around the room, at those same plants now deteriorated. 'This place, it looks just like—one of those old museum sets. What do you call them, with the taxidermy animals posed in different environments?'

'Habitat dioramas?'

'Yes—a habitat diorama.'

Apart from the easy-chairs, a tall lamp, a coffee table with a beaten-up suitcase sitting beneath, and the plants, the room was empty—but that crowd of plants! Even as yellow and sick as they looked, they were bursting out of their coloured pots like they'd been plugged into the electrical sockets.

'I tidied up a little. I'm glad you called first.'

'No problemo.' Aidan smiled thinly. 'I hope you don't mind if I say this, but I noticed when I came in—I'm not sure—it smells like maybe something's stuck—in the walls?'

Bryce drained his tea. 'It's an old building. Plenty of avenues for rats to find their way in. I hear them now and then. One or two may not have found their way back out.'

'It's not awful or anything, but it's there—or have I got a faulty nose?'

'I noticed something a while ago.' Bryce waved a hand under his nostrils and drew in a stream of air. 'I thought the problem had been fixed. I must have just grown used to it.'

'I know a guy, an exterminator. He *fixed* a whole kingdom of rats at my folks' house, out in the wop-wops. Rats, possums, feral cats. It's a lot for the two of them to keep on top of.'

'I'll mention it to the landlord—to mention it to the body corp. They've been struggling with a similar ant problem.'

Aidan spread his arms out, the mug dangling from two fingers, and sighed. 'I miss James so damn much.'

'If only it wouldn't take so long to stop hurting, right?'

'I'm sorry, Bryce. You must be—'

'Yes. I miss June very much. It's a shame about you and James.'

'I hadn't realised things were still so rough for you. I'm sorry about it, Bryce.'

'It's fine. Things—they're improving.'

'You can't always tell with people, can you? I thought James would never leave me, and I'd thought you were—everything considered—doing okay. You seemed, last year, like you'd stepped out of your grief and made peace with June going.'

'At times, I perhaps felt peaceful. But I never made peace.'

'I should shut my big mouth.'

'It's fine, Aidan. What I mean is, I never faced up to the certainty of her being gone. It only truly sunk in towards the end of the year, heading into Christmas. June had rather pagan tendencies, and tried to filter out the rest. But the regular festivities only made me think of her more, and then I found myself on black ice. To begin with, though, the reality of her being gone, it wasn't a reality I shared. I used to pretend it never happened.'

'As in, denial?'

'It was a kind of useful game, at first. And it wasn't so hard. You won't know this, but we were meant to go tramping *together* that day. It was a new trail for us, supposedly easy, but with an overnight camp. We'd packed everything up the day before—we were always prepared, in that sense. But in the morning, we had a fight—a grumpy, pointless fight. I'd asked June to air out the mattress rolls, and she hadn't. "If you thought of doing it," she said, "then why didn't you just go ahead and do it?" I told her I had other things to get done. Never mind all the back and forth, it doesn't matter now. The point is, things escalated. We'd been drinking, and we were tired and hungover. Not awful, but worse than we should have been. The fact of that was a stress on both of us. Why hadn't we stopped ourselves, or stopped each other, from having one more glass? Well, I told June, after this long row, that we may as well forget the whole trip. Didn't we both have better things to do than spend time alone with someone we couldn't stand? Of course, I didn't mean it, though it felt like I did at the time. June, she was always very forthright. She decided to head off on her own. Even though the trail was easy, I worried something would go wrong, and I became convinced that she'd feel the same way and would turn the car around and come home. I distracted myself as best I could for the afternoon, and did a good job of it, because dusk and darkness came along quickly. Then I knew that she'd done it. I won't repeat what the waiting was like, that next twenty-four hours, how it was to call the police, and what the next bit of waiting was like after that. You were witness to a moment of it. But the fact is, I kept on waiting. That's what I mean, that I pretended it never happened. I kept on waiting. I somehow thought she was still out there, walking through the bush. I thought, She'll come back in her own good time, I've just got to wait.'

'I remember your speech at the wake. It was short, so not a lot to remember. You said that part of you hoped they'd never find her. It confused me at the time, but I guess I understand now.'

Bryce said, 'Tell me if this sounds crazy.'

'Sure,' Aidan said. 'Shoot. Let me hear it.'

'I have a dreadful fear of misremembering her, of getting some detail wrong. I see her everywhere. But is my memory letting her down? I can't be sure of the parts I keep picking up and trying to put back together. I had a thought, that she used to put chilli jam on her food. And yet, another thought reminds me that she couldn't handle the slightest bit of spice. Can both be true? It sounds silly, but I worry about it immensely.'

Aidan thought of the conversation he had with Fiona, when he told her he'd be visiting Bryce, and she had declined to join him. I have a feeling as if I'm somehow responsible, she'd said. It's been working away at me. I know I haven't done anything wrong, but I feel as if I'm a source of interference disrupting a pattern. I don't think it would be good for him if I came.

'That doesn't sound crazy to me. Sometimes the brain is like a kaleidoscope,' Aidan said, and noticed a smile pass across Bryce's lips. Had Fiona also provided this snippet of conversation to Bryce previously? If she had, at least it brought her, another friend, briefly into the room, which Aidan still felt was right. 'It's the same bits and pieces shifting around inside, but different patterns come together.'

Bryce was silent a minute.

'They never found her. I hope they will. When it happens, I'll be ready to welcome her home.'

'They're still searching?'

'The case isn't officially closed. I'm not giving up.'

'Of course. I hope it can happen soon.'

'I do too. Very much so.'

Bryce leaned back in his chair. Aidan felt watched, as if the next move in a kind of game was expected of him. Was there a game being played—something more than the slow, hesitant dance of a sad conversation? The apartment seemed to shrink around him. He needed to think—he would talk this all over with Fiona. He pulled out his phone and checked the time. 'I'd better make tracks. Thanks for the excellent cup of tea, Bryce.'

Bryce stood and took their mugs to the kitchen, then walked Aidan to the front door. The rattle and buzz of the extractor fan grew louder as they passed the bathroom. Aidan paused and inhaled. It felt wrong that Bryce had ended up in a place like this. He promised Bryce he would send through the details of the exterminator.

'And I'll let Donna know you need more time.' He patted Bryce's shoulder. 'Take it easy, Bryce.'

Bryce stood aside to let Aidan pass, and Aidan opened the door and stepped into the corridor. He turned and made a last survey of the apartment. He wasn't sure if he'd come back here again. Today felt like enough—or like anything further would be too much, for him and perhaps also for Bryce. He would try to describe the place to Fiona in detail, to build a shared mental replica of the dwelling with Bryce inside it, which, he guessed, they could then study. He noticed, tucked beneath the large fronds of a fern, a pair of newly muddied hiking boots.

'Take it easy, Aidan,' Bryce said from across the threshold.

Aidan moved along the corridor to the stairwell and went

down. He emerged from the building into the car park, relieved by the open space, then stopped and looked back up at the windows, just catching sight of Bryce as he receded through the foliage, away from the glass.

It's Been a Long Time

Within the darkest recesses of the mind there exist impatient creatures that pace and growl and scrape their ragged claws across walls of bone. O! Though they may with great effort be defied or denied, and at times may withdraw and slumber, some say they can never be truly defeated, never slaughtered or banished.

Traipsing along the footpath, Emma gave the baguette a squeeze in its brown paper bag, feeling the crunch of the crust, and the yielding, yeasty flesh within. Up ahead, her apartment building squatted on the roadside. 'My wild days are over, done and dusted,' Emma said, getting used to the way the words rolled around in her mouth and then came tumbling out. 'I'm not sure I will, but thank you for offering.' Emma supposed it was like learning lines. 'O! If you're going to insist. But just one will do. Halfway is heaps. That's plenty, Paige, thank you! Just the one for me. I'm afraid I'll have to leave the rest to you.'

Waiting up ahead in her apartment, the spiced pumpkin soup was ready, the green salad was ready, the cheeses were reaching room temperature. Emma suspected she may be coeliac, yet she gripped the fresh baguette in her hand because Paige had said she would bring the wine. I will say the bread is for the soup, though it is not. 'No, I don't think I am coeliac after all. Load me up with bread, bread, bread!' Have I told Paige that I suspect I may be coeliac? It has been such a long time. Emma reached the apartment building and scuttled through the broad entryway, a stray leaf blown down from elsewhere, lost in the city. It's been a long time since I last saw any friends at all. It's been a long time since I last touched a drop—

Crunch—crunch—crunch—

But I must not wreck the baguette!

Emma pressed the button to call the lift. Its wires and gears began to squeal and groan. A civil, sociable, friendly glass of wine with lunch—just the one. It will be soaked up swiftly. I won't even feel the buzzing in my veins. 'You go ahead and finish the bottle, Paige. Just one glass is enough for me.' Emma opened the outer door of the lift, tugged aside the vintage concertina gate, stepped into the tiny mobile room and began her ascent.

Lunch would finish, and then the afternoon would begin, and then the evening would begin, and then night would begin, all of them passing softly, easily. O, but there was already the scraping of ragged claws, and the growl of unslakable wanting.

Paige was just the sort of person to invite herself round for lunch, and she had. 'Yes—it has been far too long!' Emma had screamed down the phone at Paige, who had been ringing non-stop for three whole days. 'Why, yes, of course you should bring a bottle of wine!' The words had simply escaped from her mouth, and then Paige had said, 'Perfecto, my bumpkin. Long lunch on Sunday. Ciao!' Paige was just the sort of person to turn up early, and she would. What is the time? Emma reached for her phone, patted the pockets of her jeans, scowled at her forgetful nature. Where did I leave the blasted thing—the kitchen bench. A photocopied recipe for spiced pumpkin soup concealing the phone's blank screen.

The lift squealed and groaned, then shrieked, fell half a floor and stopped violently.

Emma squawked and gasped, stumbled and dropped the baguette, trod upon the baguette, wrecked the baguette underfoot. She retreated into a corner and crouched, hands flat against the walls, ears attuned to the smallest noise.

The silence was absolute.

Emma crept forwards on her haunches and reached for the emergency button. She pressed it then released it, pressed it then released it, pressed it firmly for several long seconds then released it.

The lift squealed and groaned, shrieked and fell once more, and Emma toppled backwards, her head colliding with the handrail.

The silence was absolute.

Paige was just the sort of person who would take the stairs, and she was—bounding up two steps at a time, gripping the bottle of vodka in its brown paper bag. The occasion is worthy of a splash of the good stuff, Paige repeated in her mind. It's been such a long time. And on the off-chance that Emma prefers a gentle start, she will no doubt have a stockpile of boring old sauv blanc to sip on. It is a reasonable place to begin, in all fairness to Emma—and wouldn't it be rude to say no to a nice one.

Paige pushed open the sticking stairwell door and strode along the corridor, wiping her sweaty brow with her sleeve. O! Emma, Emma, Emma, Emma. You ought to escape from this tired old dump. The upkeep is appalling. Why do you persist here, a diamond renting amongst lumps of coal? Only, don't get any funny ideas about your childhood. Do not think of returning to the countryside, where I'd never see you again. Though it's been so long, maybe you've forgotten why you were once so glad to greet the city. 'Emma, hello-o-o-o,' Paige called, tapping Emma's door with the heavy bum of the vodka bottle. She rapped louder, using her knuckles. 'Emma, hello-o-o-o.'

The silence was absolute.

Paige reached for her phone. She called Emma's number and heard another phone ringing inside the apartment. It rang and rang and rang until it went to voicemail: '*This is Emma, I'm battling my demons in the smouldering pits of hell right now, so please leave a message and I will get back to you.*' Paige hung up and wondered if her friend Emma, who she hadn't seen in a terribly long time, was in trouble. Passed out in the bath, perhaps—it had happened before. The incident had so frightened Paige that she now only took showers. Emma was the same. They both had learned. More likely, Emma had popped down to the bakery to pick up some fresh bread rolls, or perhaps a baguette. She had said soup was on the menu, and what is soup without fresh bread rolls, or perhaps a baguette?

Or had Emma said she was first going to have breakfast downtown with that strange one, Judy? In which case, bacon and eggs and bubbly would be casually, joyfully ingested while the conversation swung and drifted, and time gently slipped away.

Paige lowered herself down to sit on the dusty carpet, resting her bony spine against Emma's door.

After a little while there came dimly from the back of her mind the scraping of ragged claws, a salivating growl. Paige shrugged and murmured something to herself. Then with a crack she uncapped the bottle of vodka and continued the process of waiting.

A Spare Room

Thursday, 11:40am. Melati crossed the worn grey carpet towards the desk where a woman was seated with her hands clasped beneath her chin. There were five piles of paper stacked on the desk, irregularly spaced and at angles to one another. What did the arrangement mean? One pile of applications yet to be assessed, another of those approved, another of those denied—but then what else, and then what else? The top pages were smothered in indecipherable sticky notes. As Melati drew nearer, she noticed ballpoint and highlighter pens scattered amongst the piles of paper like insects scuttling between tall nests. A takeaway coffee cup sat atop a flattened, grease-stained paper bag. The woman was young—half Melati's age at most. Melati wondered if she was the gatekeeper to someone older and more senior.

'Please,' the woman said, unclasping her hands and indicating the empty seat opposite her. She offered a smile—a polite gesture, clearly rehearsed but welcoming. The woman's role must require a sympathetic ear. And surely she had some degree of influence—even if the final, crucial decisions were not hers to make.

This stage of the process would be a matter of arming this young woman with information, so that she could negotiate on Melati's behalf. An advocate—well, that was acceptable.

Melati removed her backpack and sat down. The mossy padding of the seat felt damp. She pulled off her gloves and slipped a hand beneath her and discovered that the seat was dry. Her face flushed. She wanted the interview to go smoothly—to not be deceived or dismissed—yet already she had made an error.

'How are you?' the woman asked.

'I am all right, thank you,' Melati said, placing her gloves in a side pocket of her backpack. 'I'm looking for a new place to live.'

'May I ask your name?'

'Jasmine.'

'And your surname?'

The woman didn't seem annoyed about having to prompt her, but Melati registered her omission as another error, and the backs of her hands prickled. She mustn't get in her own way. Or was it in the atmosphere, the cause of that feeling on her hands? It was good to be in from the cold, but the air conditioning, as well as heating the space, seemed to be sucking out the moisture. Did this woman feel it, slowly drying out like a salted fish in her office all day? Surely not. The prickling sensation was perhaps due only to the temperature shift, going from outside to inside, taking the gloves off.

'Henderson,' Melati said.

The woman shook her computer mouse and the screen flared into life. 'I'm Ruth. You're looking to be placed in a council property?'

Melati nodded.

'Do you have your application form and some ID?' Ruth mournfully regarded the piles of paper on her desk.

'I was hoping to have a talk first.' Another form would be the last thing Ruth needed.

'We'll be able to talk as we go along,' Ruth said. With a ballpoint pen she pointed at a clock on the wall.

Melati's face flushed again. There were steps that Ruth needed to take and time she had to keep, and Melati should follow her lead. She lifted her backpack onto her knees, unzipped the rear pocket and extracted the manila folder. She slipped out her application form and passport, and leaned across the desk, meeting Ruth halfway.

'Thank you,' Ruth said, taking the documents, and Melati caught the faint scent of bitter coffee on her breath.

'You must be very busy,' Melati said.

'Up to here,' Ruth said, a hand to her forehead like a salute, as she sat back down.

She held the passport open on the desk with one hand and with the other she pinched a corner of the form's cover page, as though handling something dirty or delicate, and flipped past it to reveal the information overleaf. She looked from the form to the passport and back again.

'This has a different name,' she said. 'Melati?'

'My Indonesian name.'

Her husband had suggested she adopt an Anglo name to help those in her new country who would be unlikely, he said, to adapt on her behalf. The translation had preserved something in the compromise. From Melati to Jasmine, the names linked by the scent of the white flower.

'I see here that you were born in Indonesia.'

'Yes. But I'm a citizen of only New Zealand. The Indonesian government cancelled my citizenship. They don't allow people to be citizens of Indonesia and another country.'

'I'll have to update your Given Name,' Ruth said, scribbling on the form. 'But I'll note Jasmine as your Preferred Name.'

Ruth slid the passport back across the desk and Melati returned it to the safety of her backpack.

'You've lived in New Zealand a while?'

This surprised Melati. Not the question itself, but the sudden lift in Ruth's voice, the warmth with which she asked. It suggested an interest beyond the strict requirements of the interview—perhaps a willingness to help. As if she wished to encourage this optimism, Ruth raised her hands, ballpoint poised between two fingertips, and said, 'Tell me about that.'

Melati's lips were dry and sticking to her teeth. She ran her tongue across her teeth, over her lips. How was Ruth unaffected by the quality of the air?

'I met my husband in Indonesia forty-five years ago. He was teaching English, working under the Colombo Plan. He came often into my father's shop, where I worked with my sister and brother. When he finished his programme and returned home, we kept in touch, sending postcards and letters. Then we decided I should visit New Zealand for a holiday—so we saved and divided the cost. Soon after, he proposed marriage. I obtained my work visa and stayed a year. Then we travelled to Indonesia to get married, but came back here to live.'

Melati paused to swallow. She thought of telling Ruth about her family's nervous joy, and how her fiancé and his diffident parents had been guided through the wedding ceremony. She thought of telling how, six months after she arrived back in New Zealand, she received a phone call from her father, his sombre voice rendered more remote by the crackling connection. He said that her brother was perhaps in truth a foolish communist, but he didn't think so. He said regardless, her brother had been murdered, his body found abandoned in a muddy tributary. Don't come home, her father said. It is not safe. She would have, however, if she could have afforded a return trip to Indonesia so soon.

Instead, the death of her brother became her first great loss, felt more sharply for her new-found sense of isolation.

Ruth flipped ahead to Partner Information. She looked up at Melati, eyebrows raised.

'My husband passed away,' Melati said. 'Three years ago.'

'I'm sorry. You live by yourself?'

Ruth's voice had cooled.

It was true, Melati knew, that the mention of a troubling thought can cause another person to retreat. Sometimes it was a physical removal, or only a retreat into themselves, as Ruth was doing. In situations like this, at least, she could watch it happening. With some people, though, you never knew they had pulled away, until one day you realised they were not coming back.

'I have an apartment,' Melati said.

'The same place you lived with your husband?'

'No. We had a house.'

'You owned a house?'

'We rented. It was too expensive by myself once he was gone. So after a year, I began looking for a new place. I found my apartment in the summer, but in the winter it gets very cold. I complain to the property manager, but they do nothing. The landlord still increases the rent. Every year they increase the rent.'

As if responding to some internal cue, Melati's nose began to run. She removed a handkerchief from her jacket pocket and wiped first one nostril then the other.

'You have no heating?'

'I have an oil heater.'

'Do you use it often?'

'Yes.' Ruth opened her mouth to speak, but Melati continued. 'I put the heater in the lounge, but the lounge is open to the kitchen and hall, so the heat goes out. Sometimes I put the heater in the bedroom and shut the door, and that's how I stay warm.' Melati stuffed the handkerchief back into her pocket.

'I only meant to check.' Ruth shifted in her seat.

Melati had put her on the back foot, but it didn't feel like an advantage. Ruth's voice sounded even flatter and colder than before.

Ruth turned another page.

'You're on the pension?'

'It's not much.'

'And you have no other source of support?'

Melati thought of the dairy near the house where she and her husband had lived for thirty years. All that time, the same man had worked at the dairy. The three of them had become friendly across the counter, the experience of getting older shared through the casual intimacy of so many small interactions.

Melati's whole mouth was dry now and her skin was tightening. As the sound of the ticking clock became sharply audible, she realised that it was not the air conditioning that was causing her dehydration but the room itself, the arrangement of planes and objects—the clock on the butter-yellow wall, the piles of paper, the grey computer—and Ruth and herself two lumps amongst it all. It was an environment designed to take before it would give, and Melati's body could not help but respond to that demand at a base level.

'No. Not really,' Melati said. 'No income.'

'No, or not really?'

'Not anymore.'

She could feel her throat closing up, choking off the memory.

Talking might recalibrate the balance of the room. If the room wanted things from her, and if she gave them over, then the room might give her what she had entered it to obtain. Ruth was the room's ears. But was she listening? What if Melati's talking encouraged the return of that earlier moment, when it had seemed that Ruth's interest briefly expanded beyond the parameters of the room?

'I worked at a dairy,' Melati said. 'A month after my husband's funeral, I went to the dairy for milk. The owner asked if I would watch the store while he ran errands. He said he'd be gone only fifteen minutes and would pay me ten dollars. I agreed and he showed me how the till works—not so different from my father's. A few people came along, but I had no problems. It was like the old days. The owner returned and told me I did a good job. He paid me the ten dollars and didn't charge me for the milk. The next time I went there, he asked if I'd watch the till again, this time for an hour. After that, I started watching the till for one hour, twice a week.'

'Pocket money,' Ruth said. 'Don't worry about disclosing it.'

Ruth was smiling but she hadn't listened at all.

'I don't go now. I stopped once I moved into my apartment.' Melati ran her fingers across the papery skin of her palms. 'Is there any water?'

'Oh. Sure.' Ruth pointed with her pen. 'Out and to the right.'

Melati stood and left the room. The air in the larger lobby had decidedly more moisture in it—apparent in the taste of a single breath—but Melati still felt dried up, like an insect husk. She filled a paper cup from the cooler and returned to the room. She sat in the mossy seat and sipped from the cup until it was empty. She wanted to say that the routine of leaving her house to watch the till and offer the people from her neighbourhood the simple things they needed— bread and milk and ice cream and birthday cards—had, in the eighteen months following her husband's death, helped keep her mind in the world. Then she had moved out of the house and into the apartment. The 'pocket money' from the dairy had been useful, but it had mattered less than another person understanding what she needed at a time when she hadn't understood it herself.

'You okay?' Ruth asked.

'Yes,' Melati said. 'I wanted to ask about visitors.'

Ruth glanced again at the clock. 'We have a few more eligibility questions to get through. I see you've got something in savings.'

'Not much.' Melati placed the empty cup on the desk and the sound of its hard-edged bottom against the wood surprised her. It felt like a small but compulsive act of violence. 'I add some of my savings to my pension, to help pay the bills.'

'And no children?'

'My husband has one daughter. She lives in the UK.'

'What's your relationship like with her? Sorry, I have to ask.'

'Her mother used to talk in her ear when she was young. I don't think the daughter believes her now, but too many years have passed.'

'Do you have other family in New Zealand?'

'My family is in Indonesia.'

'How about on your husband's side?'

'He has a sister, in Invercargill. The sister . . .'

'Yes? Tell me.'

The sister was one of the reasons Melati had started looking for somewhere new to live—weeks ago, before she'd even considered council housing as an option. There had been pragmatic and understandable reasons why the sister had stopped visiting, or so Melati had thought. But now she wondered—and was this an effect of the room and the subtle way it positioned her differently in relation to her own life?—whether the reasons had masked a deeper desire to withdraw, just the same as some of the others, people who were close to her husband, had withdrawn.

'I want to know about visitors,' Melati said.

'Okay. In what way?'

'Can visitors stay in council places?'

'Sure. As long as they don't stick around long term. The tenant is responsible for any guests, if they cause damage or whatever.'

'The sister used to visit each year. At the house, she stayed in the spare room. My husband—he filled it up, with computers and books and things all over the shelves and table. But there was enough space for a bed. She stayed one time in the house after he was gone. With my apartment, there is no spare room and the sister is too old to sleep on the couch. She has stayed in a hotel, but it's too expensive. Now, this year the sister tells me she won't visit anymore.'

'You want somewhere with a second bedroom?'

'Yes.'

'Does anybody other than your sister-in-law visit?'

'Yes, local friends. Nobody outside Wellington. Nobody stays.'

'Two-bedroom places attract higher rent.'

'My apartment is already expensive. A council place will be cheaper.'

'We have a shortage. There's a lot of demand for housing. Families with nowhere to go. We're struggling to find places for them all. Sometimes they've got their kids sleeping in the living room. We're not supposed to allow that, but it's better than sleeping in a car.'

'There are no places with a spare room?'

'Not right now. Any that come up are reserved for families.' Ruth looked at the piles of paper. 'We're totally chocka and it breaks my heart to say so. But I will absolutely put you on the list and we'll stay in touch.'

A moment of silence passed. Ruth looked again at the clock, then set down her ballpoint pen, and Melati understood it was over. She stood and put on her backpack, one strap and then the other. She walked out of the office, knowing that, while she had thanked Ruth, it was rude that she'd left her empty cup on the desk, but also knowing none of it mattered. What good were rules when the rules demanded she become so much worse off before she'd be deserving of help? And why couldn't Ruth find some way to help, regardless of the rules? Perhaps Ruth had spent too much time in that fucking room. Or perhaps some people never listened—all they ever heard was noise.

Thursday, 11:40am. Ruth wondered about going for a drink after work. A new beer bar had opened and her flatmate Natasha said the levels of kitsch were about right in this one. Plenty of pop-culture figurines secreted in corners that people would stumble across and shout through the noise to their friends, 'Can you believe it, it's the Millennium Falcon!' Ruth reached for the phone in her desk drawer, but she paused when she noticed her next client shuffling in. She reconfigured her body into a professional and welcoming pose. This client moved like all the others. Even the ones as young as Ruth and younger shuffled, it was that kind of social affliction. It made people ashamed and their shame showed in how they moved, in the surreptitious way they looked down at the world's feet. Ruth was starting to really dislike the sight of them. Over a beer with Natasha she'd say, 'To be honest, it's getting so that I can't stand looking them in the face day after day. I can't stand saying over and over again that I'm super sorry, but I just can't give you what you need.'

Ruth told the client to take a seat. She had a compact backpack in reasonable condition, as was her clothing. A puffer jacket, tidy blouse and black pants. Woollen scarf, lightly pilled. A knitted hat with a pattern of a cat's face— black whiskers and a triangle nose, pink bits in the ears. Pretty cute hat. Ruth would've liked one for herself. She couldn't be too hard up against it, dressed in decent-enough threads. Ruth looked through her paperwork. Indonesian, late sixties, widowed. Right off the mark she fitted one of the priority categories: able-bodied elderly. She'd still be near the bottom of the pile. She already had a private rental and she wasn't in debt.

Ruth hadn't stretched since breakfast and her chair was uncomfortable and felt a little damp. She slipped a hand under her butt to check. Nothing. Maybe her body was just going numb. That was the way of things lately—stuck sitting for hours on end.

The client's rental sounded no worse than the council's housing stock, which was to say that few homes in Wellington were pleasant during the winter, or any season. Even with a good bit of morning sunlight, Ruth's rental got mouldy. It was built into a bank and surrounded by bush. You had to run a dehumidifier ten months out of twelve. Lots of places were like that. The client's landlord was stonehearted, and of course the rental agent was only working for the person who paid them. Ruth dealt with her landlord direct and the lease was under her name. It helped that the landlord knew who she was—it meant she was harder to ignore. There'd been no movement on getting a heat pump installed, though. Keeping the place warm would help with the ceiling mould, which she and Natasha had to clean off every six months using chemicals that somehow never killed all the spores. Ruth made a mental note to offer the client a couple of brochures at the conclusion of the interview: 'Tenants' Rights' and 'Tips to Help Keep Your Home Warm and Dry'.

The client's main deal was that she wanted someone to talk to. Ruth was happy to lend an ear, but the clock was ticking. Volumetric reporting was part of her reality. Assisting as many people as possible. They were halfway through the interview, but they had used up three quarters of their time. Listening to clients helped put things in perspective, though. You had to leave your own shit at home, but you couldn't help drawing comparisons. Ruth's problems weren't a scratch on her clients'. She could cover her rent without trouble. Her flatmate was her best friend. She drank thirteen-dollar bottles of wine and ate fresh fish once a week. She had high-speed unlimited internet access and streamed content constantly. These things weren't luxuries—they were only the baseline of modern living. The cost of getting ahead was much higher. Home ownership was somewhere in Ruth's future, but in the meantime, she'd have to keep paying down her landlord's mortgage, and she'd need a new job. Maybe something in finance or marketing. Something that paid better than it should, where the work was more abstract and kept the unpleasantness of the world at a distance. Maybe

Ruth and Natasha could buy a house together. They could pool their resources, get on the ladder, climb to the top of the heap, build an empire, live like queens.

Listening for sustained periods was difficult, like holding a squat. Ruth could feel her language hardening as she spoke, could feel her body crimping into postures she knew would appear defensive. It was an automatic response. If only people like this client were more deserving of their circumstances. Some people brought their problems on themselves—or at least they didn't help themselves. But this client had done nothing wrong. It wasn't the saddest story Ruth had heard that morning, but it stung like they all stung. Ruth collected these stories like needles in her heart. She told the client that she'd do what she could. At the very least, she'd touch base in a few months to see if her needs had changed.

Ruth watched the client walk away. Her backpack bobbed in rhythm with her steps, which had a bounce to them, now that she had a spark of hope. Was it misplaced, that hope? Everybody's life becomes a disaster eventually. Dilapidation was simply the way of things. The trick was to hold it off as long as you could, then find a soft patch of dirt in the rubble to lie down on, until the ground finally opened up and swallowed you. Natasha had trained as an aeronautical engineer and enjoyed declaring to Ruth that life always played true to the second law of thermodynamics. Disorder always defeats order in the long run. She'd even named her pet turtle 'Chaos', thinking of the fable with the hare, although that had involved a tortoise. Chaos was still a baby, or a teenager—it was difficult to gauge. Sometimes, after parties, when it was safe to let him out of his tank, they'd tie a ribbon around his stumpy body, leading up to one of the many brightly hovering helium balloons. Ruth wondered what would happen if someone took Chaos out while a party was in progress. Partygoers loved watching him sleeping or chewing on a lettuce leaf inside his heated glass house. But seeing him roam around the floor tethered to a balloon was unbeatable. What if he got stepped on, lost amongst the confusion of balloons? Ruth wondered— only idly, not seriously—if it would make more of a brittle crunching or a hard cracking sound.

She was grinding her foot into the carpet beneath her desk. Fuck. She wasn't into animal cruelty. She never even ate chicken or pork or shrimp. No factory-farmed animals. She just needed a new job. One that didn't constantly layer up other people's problems, while she had to sit there pretending like she had no problems of her own, or like her problems had been temporarily relocated. She needed to eat a fucking sandwich. And she needed that beer and for the weekend to begin, pronto.

Ruth dragged open her desk drawer, took out her phone. She looked into its smooth obsidian surface. Her head and shoulders, reflected through greasy finger smears, were forced into silhouette by the bright bar of fluorescence suspended from the ceiling above her. She appeared obscure and tenuous. A shadow, inexplicably detached from its object, that would vanish should that bar of light blink out.

Ruth's heart thumped against her ribcage. She hadn't passed the client either of the brochures. She looked up, but the compact backpack and cute cat hat were already out of sight.

The Ether of 1939

I dug around, once it looked like I wouldn't be moving on from this time anytime soon . . . I'm glad, too. Now that I have you . . . No, not exactly. I've never had reason to take an especially personal interest in the deep past before. There are two threads that connect, as it turns out. There's the apartment block's history, and a family lineage . . . Yes, a fairly distant relative. Take a look at this . . . It's a scrapbook I started. A place to collect stories, or their spectral traces . . . Well, stories are a time-travel device in their own way. Like reaching into a version of the past or future, or a parallel moment of the present . . . This clipping's what I wanted to show you. It's an old newspaper advert . . . That's right. They built radios here, in the 1930s and 40s, long before the building was converted into apartments. That distant relative of mine worked at the radio factory. It's an unusual story. There was a dreadful incident involving a boy named Greg Ford . . . Hold on and I'll tell you. For many years, people thought the place was haunted . . . It's partly why the building later sat abandoned for so long. Maybe it still is haunted. It could be the wicked weather outside, but I do feel a slight chill . . .

DOMINION 14 AUG. 1939

— CAPITAL RADIOS —

Proudly presents

THE HOME THEATRE ALL-WAVE CONSOLE

Featuring
Hand-carved cabinetry boasting surrounding details of a sublime theatrical setting—see the proscenium arch, the wings, and backstage!

With
High-precision tuning and an immaculate tone, thanks to the very finest in radio technology available to-day (including 22 valves and twin moving coil speakers).

—

Experience radio entertainments with all the spirit and liveliness of the theatre, from the convenience and comfort of your fireside.

—

£68 / 10 / -

**Made in Wellington
Dist. around N.Z.**

For pre-orders and literature contact:
Capital Radios, Wellington

*
**

On Friday morning, in the office on the factory's third floor, Geoffrey Merchant told Jack Newman there were two things that worried him: rumours of a supernatural connection with the new radio console, and the threat of a strike. Fortunately, he noted, the markets for radio consoles and factory labour were both in good health. Merchant owned Capital Radios and could be counted amongst those businessmen who had managed to turn a profit during the Depression. Jack was the factory foreman, forty-one years old, tall and broad-chested, though few people considered him imposing. The factory hands respected Jack as much for his keen appreciation of what was fair as for his competence as an electrical engineer.

It was Jack's job to return the factory floor to full production.

'The hands are frightened half to death,' Jack said. He stood, head bowed, a few steps back from Merchant's desk. 'Perhaps the thunder and lightning didn't help.'

'Which of them are resisting? The unionists?' Merchant asked.

The uneasy murmurs of a contingent of engineers and carpenters could be heard through the thin office wall, coming from the adjacent electronics assembly room.

'Not only them,' Jack said. 'All the hands are spooked. Several were nearby and heard the broadcast. They vouch that young Gregory's name was mentioned and that his death was predicted.'

The lines of Merchant's face lengthened and he drummed on the desktop with his fingers. 'How is the boy holding up?'

*
**

They produced the last great New Zealand radio—the Home Theatre console. It was a master craft. Quite large. Antique sets can sell for several hundred dollars. Auction houses are interesting places to get a sense of present ideas about the past . . . I don't know. Technology that really changes people's lives tends to become ubiquitous . . . Planned obsolescence is a trend in the current period, I've noticed . . . Yeah, it was tempting to bid for one . . . In my future? Time-travel tech— all that infrastructure, and the portable machine, the injected chronochips—it's very costly. Definitely not ubiquitous. And not always reliable . . . Good question. I'm not sure precisely when it was first developed.

^
**

Jack said he'd shout the factory's three leading hands —Peter, Walt, Edwin—a round of beer at the Open Arms when the factory closed for the day. Peter led the electrical engineers, taking the job over from Jack when he was promoted to foreman. Walt had been employed at the factory for four years, leading the team of carpenters for the last two. Edwin had travelled up from Otago the year before and was the newest and, in his mid-twenties, the youngest of the leading hands. He and an Irishman of the same age made up the design team, and Edwin also managed the two sales staff.

Peter helped Jack carry their last glasses of beer to the corner where Walt and Edwin were huddled. The pub was crowded with workers from the neighbourhood drinking their fill before home, though the din of their lubricated conversations meant Jack and his team could talk freely.

'Mr Merchant says he's prepared to replace any hands that want to see out their month's notice, or those who might otherwise want to forfeit a month's pay and depart immediately,' Jack said, and took a large sip of his beer. 'A few of the workers overheard the discussion. They'd scarpered before I left Merchant's office, but word will get around quickly. I'll be surprised if any of them decide to tempt fate. But just in case—talk with as many of your hands as you can and make sure everyone's on the floor on time come Monday morning.'

'I say Merchant's all steam,' Edwin said. 'Interest is already mounting. The sample console in the showroom's getting tarnished from the attention it's receiving. I suggested to Merchant that we put a card on it: PLEASE REFRAIN FROM TOUCHING. But he loves that people can't help themselves, even if it's just an empty shell—a beautifully sculpted empty shell, of course, Walt. Merchant can smell the money. He needs everyone on board.'

Jack nodded. 'It's probably a bluff, but let's not call him on it. He's still the boss and can make life tougher than it needs to be.'

'What about Gregory?' Walt said.

'Gregory is excluded,' Jack said.

'Fifty-eight men and women in my team,' Peter said. 'I can't be expected to herd that many frightened sheep.'

'They'll calm down,' Jack said. 'And I plan to take a look at the prototype myself, see what might have happened. Though I suspect a radio play got the better of Gregory's imagination. Who knows what reason the other hands had to make it a game.'

'You give what they said no credit at all?' Edwin said.

'I'm giving all options credit,' Jack said. 'That includes

the option of a boy's imagination being provoked.'

Edwin stared into his glass. 'I don't know if it's a ghost we've got, but I do believe in them. I once saw the spirit of my grandfather when I was a boy. He'd been helping one of my uncles clear some bush when he was crushed by a felled tree. Night of his funeral, he appeared in my bedroom doorway. His body was uninjured, looking the same as he always had. He didn't say a word. Just stared in at me, then turned away and vanished. Next day, my father beat me black and blue for claiming to have seen him. He believed that no dead man ever came back unless they'd been sent by the devil himself. I think children have a special sensitivity when it comes to spirits.'

'You ever see another one?' Peter asked.

'No, thank God.' Edwin crossed himself and drank his beer.

'What about you, Walt,' Peter said. 'You got a view on the spirit realm?'

'I say my evening prayers, and I hope in the end to find myself standing in the light and not the flames,' Walt said. 'Gregory wasn't the only one who heard the broadcast, remember. Some of my carpenters were there.'

'One of my engineers as well,' Peter said. 'He swears Gregory Ford's name was spoken, and I believe him. It was no radio play.'

'If it was a ghost, then whose ghost was it?' Edwin said.

'You talk about the damned walking the earth,' Peter said. 'It could be the old tailor—the suicide.'

'In the factory?'

'It's not a popular topic of discussion,' Jack said.

'The fella who owned the factory before Merchant,' Peter said. 'He started as a boutique tailor making finery for the well-to-do. Earned a tidy sum for himself. Then he bought the factory and began mass-producing garments for the everyday man and woman.'

'Good for him,' Edwin said.

'As it so happens, he was operating the factory under sweat conditions,' Jack said.

'Aye. He managed to bribe the government inspector for a time,' Peter said. 'Till he built a habit at the poker tables that cost him more than he could pay. When he finally had to turn away the inspector's greasy paw, they threatened to expose him. One of his factory girls found him hanging from a rafter by a knotted silk dress. The business and assets were left to his wife. His nose always out for a bargain, Merchant purchased the building and land from the grieving widow for a shameful price. If a ghost was looking to take revenge on a man's business, it would be the tailor's.'

'Merchant would harangue the poor soul till it went cowering back to its grave,' Edwin said.

'The factory has a troubled history,' Walt said. 'The large consoles we're building, the one the broadcast came over— the carvings on its cabinetry are inspired by the factory's past life as a theatre, are they not? Wasn't it gutted by fire?'

'"Inspired" is the right word,' Edwin said. 'The real theatre was more modest than our designs show, I believe. No formal orchestra pit, for one thing.'

'That's true,' Jack said. 'It was a good playhouse, but not terribly elaborate. I saw one or two performances there. I'm glad the façade survived the fire at least, and that something was made of it, rather than it being torn down.'

'It lends some drama to the factory,' Edwin said. 'The masks moulded above the entranceway, they remind me our line of work's in making and selling dreams—or dream-machines.'

'Those masks are grotesque,' Peter said. 'Like a pair of deranged souls.'

'Was anybody harmed in the fire?' Walt said.

'Well, there was a rumour,' Peter said.

'Not one worth repeating,' Jack said.

'Nobody was reported dead,' Peter said. 'But a story went around about the old fella who managed things backstage. He had his adult son with him. The son had an unfit brain and couldn't be left alone. His father's presence was the only thing that kept him calm, so the old fella took him everywhere he went.'

'You know this story's a terrible lie,' Jack said.

'What happened?' Edwin said. 'Let him tell it, Jack.'

'The old fella saw an opportunity to be relieved of his burden,' Peter continued. 'As the flames were licking the curtains of the stage, he thumped his son unconscious. Left him to perish, then stumbled out into the smoke-filled night asking if anyone had seen his dear boy. Even managed to shed a few tears. Well, as the story goes, the miserable child killer started hearing his dead son's voice shortly before his own sudden expiration. Supposedly the son—wanting some company, or perhaps revenge—came and took his father with him into the great beyond.'

'How awful,' Edwin said. 'I wish you hadn't told it.'

'It's a lie. The son died of natural causes—he'd always been sickly, that's true—and his father died a few weeks later from sheer heartbreak,' Jack said. 'Now, you all know I'm spiritual enough to attend church most Sundays. But I'm not an especially devout believer in haunted furniture. I'm going to find out what's really got Gregory shook up.'

'I thought you were giving everything credit,' Peter said.

'Where it's due.'

The four men fell silent, the pub humming around them. Edwin flicked his half-empty glass with a fingernail.

'The new beacon up the coast,' he said, 'by the swimming beach. What's the place called?'

'Tītahi Bay.' Walt shook his head. 'Curious part of the coast. Back in the day, whalers from my family worked those waters. It's what brought them all the way out here, to New Zealand.'

'What on Earth possessed them?' Edwin said.

'Misplaced sense of adventure from hearing too many stories,' Peter said.

'There's an old stone not far from there—I saw it as a boy,' Walt said. 'An anchor stone. Left by a man who journeyed to these shores long before my forefathers washed up on the sand, waterlogged and worn out from hunting lamp oil.'

'Walter, I believe your family's remained waterlogged ever since,' Peter said, then clinked Walt's glass with his own and laughed. 'Sobriety's not a great strength in my line either, in fairness.'

'But we have digressed,' Walt said, looking past Peter at Edwin. 'They installed that transmitter about two years ago. The thing's large enough to broadcast into every corner of the country.'

'They caught a signal across the ditch, in Australia,' Jack said.

'It's impressive,' Walt said.

'This may sound peculiar,' Edwin said, 'but I wondered whether it might be big enough, powerful enough, to disrupt the ether.'

'Nice job, Ed,' Peter said. 'You've discovered electro-magnetism.'

'He doesn't mean electromagnetism,' Walt said.

'No,' Edwin said. 'I mean the spiritual ether.'

'You can't be too sure, I suppose,' Peter said.

'There was a real storm blowing last night,' Walt said. 'I remember it broke around the time Gregory heard the voice.'

At that moment, the barman rang the brass bell above the bar. 'Six o'clock,' he called out. 'Time, gentlemen, please.'

Only Peter joined in the three cheers that erupted across the pub.

'Jack,' Edwin said, once the crowd had quietened down. 'Why was Gregory playing with the prototype?'

'Testing the frequency range,' Jack said. 'I assigned him a few extra hours in quality assurance, for the pocket money. Now, listen to me. I'm going to keep an open mind. But these ghost stories won't help with factory morale. Understood?'

'Loud and clear,' said Walt.

'Aye,' said Peter. 'No ghosts round here.'

'Understood,' Edwin said.

Jack drained his glass and the others followed suit.

'And Peter,' Jack said, 'would you meet me on the floor a little earlier on Monday morning— say, half seven?'

Peter nodded, then someone shouted '"Auld Lang Syne"!' and the pub picked up the tune as Jack and his leading hands quietly departed.

*
**

I'm up and down. Mostly down. It could be another time-fever, another glitch. But I'm not sure. It feels different . . . More like cold sweats than that lightning heat . . . No, seeing a doctor is too risky. A hottie, blanket and lemon-honey will do the trick.

*
**

Jack caught a taxi to the house at the foot of Tinakori Hill, where Gregory lived with his mother and father. He asked the taxi driver to stop a block away. Walking along the roadside towards the house, he picked a small bouquet of wildflowers, which he presented to Gregory's mother, Dot, when she answered the door.

'Thought I'd come by to see how Gregory is,' Jack said. 'Everyone at the factory's been asking.'

Dot's face seemed paler and more drawn, and her green eyes duller, than Jack remembered. She looked at the small bouquet without accepting it, her gaze resting finally at her feet.

'He hasn't left his bed,' she said.

'I hope you don't mind my visiting,' Jack said. 'We ask all workers to provide their address. You knew Gregory had?'

Dot nodded.

'I don't know what happened,' Jack said. 'But I'll figure it out.'

'Alan's home,' Dot said.

'I'm sure Gregory will be all right,' Jack said.

Alan's loud voice sounded from inside the house. 'Who is it?'

'Gregory's not your concern,' Dot whispered to Jack. Then, turning her head, she said, 'It's Jack.'

'Dot, why don't you check on Gregory,' came Alan's voice. 'I can talk to Jack, if he wants to talk.'

'I'd hoped to see how Gregory's doing,' Jack called through the doorway.

'You'll see him when he's fit to return to work.'

'It's not that. He can take as long as he needs.'

Heavy footsteps fell across the timber floorboards. Jack scattered the flowers in the lavender hedgerow beneath the front window a heartbeat before Alan appeared behind Dot. Alan was as tall and broad as Jack, but unlike Jack he had a sharp edge that people quickly learned not to test.

'I'm happy to spell this out,' Alan said.

'We all wish Gregory well,' Jack said.

'All our son needs is to be left alone.'

Alan reached above Dot's head. She slipped under his arm and retreated, and he shut the door firmly in its frame.

With dusk closing in, Jack began walking back along Tinakori Road towards Bowen Street. Old memories played through his mind. The idea of a family had been carved out of Jack's life long before he and Dot ever met.

They had dated each other in their early twenties, when she'd worked as an operator at the Central Telephone Exchange where he was apprenticed as an electrical engineer. At the time, Jack was already drinking occasionally at the Midland Hotel, located a short walk from the exchange. The hotel's bar wasn't a rowdy place, but it possessed a vitalising energy that Jack couldn't put down to the drink alone. The bodies and conversations that filled the room seemed to charge the air. Jack had been content to let that energy slip around him like water, something clean and essential that couldn't be grasped.

When Dot first surprised Jack there, it was with two tickets to the annual summer Shakespeare performance at the repertory theatre. Jack suggested he buy them dinner beforehand, and they shared a meal at the hotel together. As his attendance there after work continued to increase, Dot joined him more often, and they'd sit and talk and watch the other patrons. Then one evening, Jack found himself admonishing Dot publicly for disturbing him when what he wanted was to simply enjoy his beer in peace, with just himself for company. His quick, angry words rattled them both, but afterwards he was relieved for having said them. And while Dot stopped her visits, Jack developed the habit of taking a seat facing the hotel's entryway.

As time steadily deepened, Jack had started to understand the private language that sat beneath the interactions of some of the hotel's patrons. It was like learning where the submerged stones were in a river by watching for patterns in the disturbances on the surface. And yet, the men who removed themselves in pairs by the internal stairwell, leading to the rooms above, appeared to Jack to be on fire, intent on plunging their bodies headlong into a cool aquifer. Some of those men had been amongst the first to approach Jack in the earlier days, when he'd thought he was watching not a coded series of performances but simply the rippling surface of aimless human excitement.

Jack continued to drink alone, allowing himself to quietly savour the sense of bubbling life inside the hotel bar, and also to forget the life beyond its doors—including the circumstances that were thickening around him and Dot. The idea, or the obligation, of marriage had begun to press upon Jack. He thought he knew the shape of a marriage from what he'd observed of other people, but he wondered how the daily substance of it ought to look and feel. He could not imagine it with real conviction or nuance. His mental pictures of a life with Dot were rough sketches in a notebook—impressions of a truer form, which itself could not be witnessed directly.

As Jack was finishing his beer one winter's evening, a man he'd briefly spoken with perhaps half a dozen times before took the seat beside his. After a few words of greeting, the man mentioned in an offhand manner that he sometimes liked to book a room upstairs. 'A quiet spot to spend a little extra time with a friend,' he said. 'Maybe a friend like you,

Jack.' The man touched Jack's hip, letting his hand linger, applying a gentle pressure before retracting it. Jack had never been so openly confronted before. Approaches were usually timid, fleeting, never physical. They could be easily disregarded with a mundane remark then put out of his mind. But this man had made sure his proposal could not be ignored, and for a long moment Jack was struck mute.

They were on the second step of the stairwell when Jack heard Dot speak his name. He turned around, a sudden dryness in his throat. She stood a few feet away. The way she held herself, her slight shoulders forward, her head bent down, she looked ashamed to be in that room filled largely with people of the opposite sex. 'It's true, then?' she said, raising her chin to look from Jack's face to the other man's and back again. It was a question that had been present between them for longer than either could have admitted. Their bitter silence seemed to acknowledge that the question was already answered, that there was nothing else to say. Dot turned to leave and Jack took a step towards her.

The man caught Jack by his arm. 'You can kick up a fuss later,' he said. 'Not here.'

Jack watched Dot move through the room and disappear out into the cold evening.

Six months later, he encountered Dot on the street. She was walking arm in arm with the man she would come to marry—Alan Ford. She was close enough that Jack could have reached out and touched the lace edging of her sleeve. Dot returned his look for an instant then passed him over as if he were any other man in the crowd. Jack understood then that Dot's apparent silence—amongst her social circle over the truth behind their separation, and the fact she hadn't reported him to the police—was conditional on a distance being maintained between them. That distance was necessary for them both. It would be necessary also for anyone Jack might ever grow close to. His real self could only exist in a world hidden beneath and separate from the larger world enjoyed by ordinary people—ordinary people like Dot and Alan.

Then, in November of 1938, Gregory Ford showed up at the radio factory, declaring that he was finished with school and eager to start work. He was fascinated with electronics and had constructed several crystal radio sets. Something about the boy's face caught Jack's attention, and he dimly registered the surname. He admitted Gregory to a week-long trial in Peter's engineering team, and at the end of it Merchant approved the boy's appointment to the payroll. It was then that Jack thought of the rich green of Dot's eyes, which her son had inherited.

The day following Gregory's appointment to staff, Jack was cutting through an alley on his walk home from the factory when he heard boot steps close behind him. Then Alan Ford had him pinned by his throat against the coarse brick wall. With his mouth so near Jack's face that Jack felt his lips graze his cheek, Alan promised to break every bone in Jack's skull if he laid one hand on his son.

In the year since, Jack had paid little attention to what Alan's threat meant for himself and worried instead whether Alan represented some unpleasantness in the boy's home. Jack hoped to provide a safe place that Gregory could feel happy returning to each day.

On the occasions when the tidal pull of sentiment either filled or emptied his heart completely, Jack would entertain the idea that Gregory might play the role of a surrogate son. A son neither real nor unreal, but a spectre of the imagination that existed in flesh and blood. Gregory was in those moments the product of an alternate biography, able to be comprehended with the clarity of a photograph, framed and hung upon the wall of some family home that Jack knew he would never obtain.

The cool evening air nipped at Jack's flesh. He turned off Bowen Street onto Lambton Quay, the house on Tinakori Road well behind him now.

He decided the wildflowers had been naïve, a mistake. How might Dot have understood the gesture? She wouldn't have thought it malicious or mocking, but had Jack seen a flicker of old shame pass across her eyes?

Winding his way down Lambton Quay, Jack saw the face of the Midland Hotel coming into view. They would have finished serving drinks, but he might still find some warmth and comfort for the night.

*
**

Change the channel . . . His job is to read the news. I wouldn't even say his opinions are amusing . . . It undermines ideas about what's possible, encouraging a kind of historical inertia . . . On television? It's not the medium for me. But you could. The written word's my medium of choice, though they all have their limitations . . . You're a terrific optimist. The status of people like us has been won and lost often enough in the past, not to mention the future . . . This channel's okay. At least cooking shows are underpinned by reality. It boils down to physics, chemistry, and culture . . . There have been definite advancements, but there's a long way to go . . . You can almost hear it. A persistent hum of abjection and violence. Progress is either an ongoing project— reframing and internalising—or it's abandoned, forgotten . . .

Oof, these cold shivers. I should troubleshoot the time machine.
Want to help with some calculations?

*
**

On Monday morning, before the hands began arriving, Jack and Peter opened the factory. They loaded the prototype into the service elevator and moved it down from the second-floor space where constructed radios were cleaned and tested to a storage room at the end of a wide corridor that ran behind the ground-floor showroom. The storage room was seldom accessed. It was where Peter kept the defective radios that customers traded in for discounts or money, which he would then resurrect or else disassemble for spare parts. With one foot, Jack pushed aside the small box of chains that pinned the door shut against the draughts that threaded through the factory. He spread a large rag on the floor to protect the underside of the radio, then he and Peter lowered the radio onto the rag, leaving enough clearance to shuffle past on either side.

Peter followed Jack out of the room, then paused and turned back. He took a large sheet down from one of the shelves, shook it out and draped it over the console, the excess fabric pooling on the dusty floor. With its height and rounded top, the covered console resembled a child playing dress-up as a ghost.

'To save it from the dust,' Peter explained.

As a sign that he credited his workers' concerns and that he intended to approach the situation with circumspection and care, Jack installed a heavy lock on the door. Its flat steel gleamed like a razorblade against the weathered skin of the wood.

'Anything needs to be moved in or out of that room,' Jack said to Peter, showing him the sole key to the lock, already strung on a piece of leather around his neck, 'you need only ask.'

'Thanks, Jack.'

Jack could see Peter was glad to be relieved of any responsibility for the radio, glad that the key wasn't hanging around his own neck.

Peter moved away down the corridor, towards the stairs that would take him up to the assembly room on the third floor. Jack walked around to the showroom off the main entrance. He waited amongst the living-room and kitchen furniture that had been interspersed with the radios constructed on the floors above.

Geoffrey Merchant arrived punctually at eight.

'You're here bright and early, Mr Newman.'

'Ready for a good day's work,' Jack said. Feeling some relief, he followed Merchant to the service elevator, which the old man preferred over the stairs. Jack had half worried that Merchant would wait near the entrance to count the hands as they filed into the building.

'Peter and Walter and Edwin share your confidence?'

'Yes. They're confident,' Jack said on faith.

'How's the prototype? I'd like to loan it to someone among the intended market. The Burtons are hosting a soirée in two weeks' time. I'm sure the console would draw the right attention from the members of their guest list.'

'We'll get it fixed,' Jack said. 'I've shut it away in the meantime. Keep it out of people's minds.'

'You won't be needing the aid of a priest in making your repairs?'

'We'll get it fixed.'

'Full steam ahead,' Merchant said. He entered the elevator and clicked the security gate into place, then eased the deadman control and began to rise through the building. Jack went outside.

Edwin soon arrived with his Irish assistant. They saluted Jack and he saluted back. The salesmen were not far behind. Then Walt turned up with three younger cabinetmakers in tow. Before long, all the remaining hands, excepting Gregory, filtered through the factory door. Jack said hello to each of them and they each said hello to Jack.

He was preparing to head back inside when he heard the dull slapping of hands against trouser fabric as someone unseen announced their presence.

'Word spread,' Peter said, stepping into the lozenge of morning light that fell across the old theatre's entrance, 'about your chat with Mr Merchant, and his threat to fire people on the spot.'

'They've had the weekend to settle down,' Jack said, feeling the sun's warm rays on the backs of his hands, on his face, cutting through the morning chill.

'They've had the weekend to enjoy the company of their families, and to think about what it means to have people who rely on them,' Peter said, leaning against the stonework of the entryway pillar. 'You hear the national broadcast?'

Jack nodded.

'The Depression's barely behind us, now there's another war ahead.' Peter looked around, then continued, his voice dampened. 'A lot of these guys would be willing to fight, of course. But some of the engineers have been wondering— if we were to build radio kit for the military, would our work here at the factory count towards the war effort? I'd say so.'

'The government said it's not interested in conscriptions.'

'They'll change their minds if they need the numbers,' Peter said. 'I thought I'd put a plan together, in any case. Something we could approach Merchant with, and then the government, if we need to. Would you back that, as foreman?'

'You've already spoken with Walt and Edwin?'

'Aye. Walt said he'll serve any way he can. And Edwin said he's prepared to fight. That surprised me. Edwin seems a little tender—a bit effete—doesn't he?'

'I wouldn't be too quick to judge,' Jack said. 'Did they agree with your proposal or not?'

'They said if it matters enough to others, then they'll back it. Will you?'

Jack turned his hands in the light. Gregory was scarcely two years off eighteen, although wars could stretch their misery out for long enough. And Peter was right about conscriptions—fighting would remain optional only if there were enough willing victims, and there never were in the end. Jack had been too young to serve in the Great War, at its start, and between his pleading mother and good fortune with the ballot, he was never dispatched once he was old enough. He lost a brother and two uncles to the frontlines. But this time around, as a fit man without a family depending on him, Jack would be high on the list. He thought he'd just as likely volunteer, if it might mean some other soul was saved from going—a soul like Gregory.

'Yes, I would,' Jack said. 'I'd support that. Now, let's get inside before Mr Merchant declares war on us personally.'

*
**

Some form of interference from the past. It's chaotic. All sorts of variables bringing different types and degrees of influence to bear on each other . . . Even allowing for all possibilities to exist, you have to grapple with your own sense of existence. If we could understand history better, we thought we could give it a well-judged nudge, like cheating at craps. Load the dice and roll again . . . No, thankfully. At a personal scale, the dice haven't come up snake eyes yet. The flux seems just enough of a disturbance to make me time-sick, for now. It'd need to be a relatively direct line of influence.

*
**

The factory was empty. Jack had told Peter, Walt, Edwin and Merchant that he'd spend an hour or two that evening taking a look at the prototype. He removed the key from around his neck and unlocked the door to the storage room, then pulled the slender chain that hung from the ceiling. Light from the overhead bulb filled the room, cutting the console's covered form with wedges of shadow where the folds in the sheet flowed.

Jack dragged the sheet aside. He pulled up the small stool that Peter used to reach the higher shelves, and sat in front of the radio. He turned the volume knob till he felt it click, and the radio gently came to life. He twisted it further, bringing the hiss of static to a crescendo. Then he navigated the wavelengths, as the speakers emitted whichever sounds the machine plucked from the air. Patterns of noise straining to become signal, private echoes of Morse code, actors performing dramatic readings, the swelling of orchestras, the calm diction of a game-show host and the excited chatter of his guests. The radio could attune to a thousand different articulations, each desiring escape from the ether, desiring entrance to the world through the portal of this intricate electric chamber. Jack settled for the moment on a concert channel. He twisted the volume knob clockwise then counterclockwise, and the sound expanded and ebbed with a fluid and transcendent resonance. The tone was as immaculate as their advertising promised and the console produced no hint of a rattle or hum. Jack returned to the tuning knob and probed the frequency range where Gregory had encountered the broadcast that augured his death. A soft patch of static tripped Jack's attention. He ran the needle back and forth, finally catching a sensitive fragment of clear sound. It settled on a man's voice.

There are some possible complications . . . It wouldn't be like dying. Not even like vanishing. I wouldn't even be a ghost in your memory. Our relationship's a very rare thing. The odds that we'd have ever met are miniscule . . . It's worth trying to save that, don't you think? Okay. Are you ready to hear this?

Jack let out a long breath. The broadcast was only a radio play after all. An obscure one, operating on an uncommon frequency, one Jack had never tuned into before, but it seemed benign.

The interference originates from here. Right beneath our feet. Within the last couple of days, in relative terms, for us. But in an entirely different year . . . In 1939. It traces back to the time of the radio factory.

Jack snapped his arm forwards. He twisted the volume knob until it was a half-degree from the off position. The broadcast played at a near whisper and Jack leaned towards the console.

He listened late into the night, not daring to even stretch his aching back should he miss a word. It was a kind of madness, what the voice spoke of—its claim that Jack's present was in fact the past, that the voice itself was being transmitted from the future.

If I travel back seventy-odd years in time . . . Yes, there's some risk, but less.

Seventy years on—that would mean a new century, a new millennium, an era beyond Jack's lifetime. The speaker of the voice sounded no older than Jack. It was a wild concept, listening to someone who—to take their claim at face value—did not yet exist. And wilder again was the suggestion that this person could move backwards through time, as easily as the driver of an automobile might change their direction of travel along a road.

Yet there was also a truthful intimacy in the voice's manner of speaking. It was as if the speaker was in a private room and Jack was listening at the door. Even as the meaning of the voice's words became more abstract and less clear, there was a thrill in the way that hearing that voice, unpretending and insistent, felt like eavesdropping.

It could be just as bad if I do nothing. If I leave the past alone, there may not be a future—not for us.

The obliqueness and sincerity of the words held Jack's attention such that the strangeness of those initial details— the mentioning of his year and location—gradually receded in his mind. This ebbing was helped by the voice's own avoidance of them, as if it too had found them shocking and was now reluctant to discuss them directly. Or was it the other presence, the voice's implied but unheard partner in the conversation, who had been shocked or upset? It was clear that the two—the speaker and this other person—were important to each other but also that their relationship was somehow under threat. It seemed to be in response to this that the voice's tone softened, even while it carried itself towards an apparent edge.

You know I can't continue forever like this. I can't stay time-sick and I can't just wait and see what happens. It will come to an end, for better or worse. I'd prefer to have some influence over which.

It was then that the first long silence of the evening occurred. The broadcast hadn't ended—no static came seeping through a fissure in the frequency—but the voice had stopped. The silence lasted several long minutes, becoming an almost physical presence, as if Jack could feel the idle air resting against the skin of his arms, hands, face. The silence was broken by the voice's calm agreement to some unheard proposition.

Yes. Okay. Yes.

Other silences came in smaller waves, after that. Small and lapping, alternated with quiet words about simpler matters. It was the denial of one thing and a return to something else—to more ordinary affairs. A dinner was eaten, a pot of tea was shared. With the foregrounding of a domestic setting, the effect of eavesdropping was almost overwhelming. Jack held the volume knob between his forefinger and thumb, preparing to force it that final degree towards the cancellation of sound, when a phrase froze him.

I'm lucky to have a man like you to share my life with. That's what I'm afraid of losing.

Jack sat unmoving, a statue of flesh, as the words *a man like you* passed across his mind, like a finger running down the spine.

The next morning, when Peter said to Jack, 'Things going all right with you?' Jack turned the question back on him, requesting an update on stock levels for parts, and production progress. Whether Peter spoke to Edwin and Walt, Jack didn't know. But neither approached him with queries regarding the prototype. 'Mr Merchant's keeping a close eye on our work,' Jack said to all three during his mid-morning rounds. 'Let's not slacken the pace.'

As the day progressed, Jack felt increasingly removed from the business of the factory. He carried out his duties as an actor might a well-rehearsed performance. It was a way simply to pass the day. At shutdown, he left Peter, Walt and Edwin to head to the Open Arms without him. He knew that, once there, the topic of the prototype would be raised, and he wasn't in a frame of mind for denying his experience with the radio. Rather, he was anxious for the experience to be repeated.

Jack unlocked the storage room and sat as he had the evening before, on the low stool in front of the console. The voice was there. The same mix of intimacy and sincerity was present but there was nothing of the outlandish threads from the previous evening. The broadcast asserted only a series of subdued domestic routines—a man in the company of another man, the two men going about their shared existence at home. Jack had forgotten his discomfort at the private nature of the voice. It was displaced by a growing belief that the broadcast was a personal offering, a gift intended for Jack. In this vision of the future—built out of the voice's words and Jack's imagined elaborations—Jack thought of himself as the voice's only intended addressee, its sole counterpart. In whispers, he responded to its questions and filled the gaps between the things it said with things of his own. He improvised a small life with the voice, until it told him it was time for bed. Jack listened as the silence of its sleep overtook the airwaves, while outside the factory a drunkard shouted at the stars, a stray dog howled, and the wind began to thrash.

Jack returned to the storage room each evening that week. The radio's waking dream blossomed, even while the mist of it was disturbed a handful of times when the factory was mentioned, in connection with an event that seemed, in some unclear though adverse way, to affect the speaker—the man who claimed to be living in the future.

The fantasy was too enticing, sweet, satisfying for Jack to allow it to disperse during those evening hours. It offered a vision, rendered in candid detail, that Jack knew was unattainable within the routine spaces that persisted beyond the storage-room door. Shut away at the end of the ground-floor corridor, hunched in front of the quietly playing radio, the idea that Jack might ever make a home with someone was transformed from something preposterous and obscene into something achievable, perhaps even ordinary.

During the daylight hours, spent away from the realm of the radio, the idea was harder to maintain. Life was bursting with reminders of what was real. Part of Jack's mind remained fixed on the end of each day when he could be alone with the voice, but he could not avoid the central, troubling questions about the broadcast. The factory was growing restless with the need for answers.

For the broadcast to mention the factory and the year of Jack's present, to have suggested a worker was in jeopardy, and to tailor its themes to a secret such as Jack's—these details were dangerously specific, and the threat of an intentional scandal crept into Jack's thoughts.

But who might execute such a plan?

Jack guarded his secret well, though of course other people knew it. Foremost were the men that Jack had been with—at the Midland Hotel and in the shadows of the wharves and the city's green belt. But if they were to expose Jack's secret, they also risked exposing their own. For them, the stakes were high and the gains were nil, as far as Jack could tell.

Then there was Dot—and through her, perhaps Alan. Yet, despite the hurt he had caused her, Dot had protected Jack's secret for two decades. The idea of creating a ruckus was out of character for Dot, who didn't like to interfere, who preferred to cut ties. And would even Alan go so far, to justify some sort of retaliation? It was absurd, but nonetheless, heading home those nights, Jack anticipated the sound of boot steps, the crush of fingers closing around his throat, a blow to his skull, fulfilling the promise Alan had made in the alleyway the winter before.

Or else, might someone from the factory be responsible? Jack could see no reason for the hands to feel ill will towards either Gregory or himself, but a little over seventy workers were employed at the factory and he couldn't say absolutely that none amongst them was nursing some grievance. To head off the possibility and dampen the spread of gossip, Jack told Peter, Walt and Edwin that he suspected an ill-conceived practical joke after all, and that he hoped whoever was responsible would step forward—if they wanted to be treated with any leniency. The leading hands made sure the report was heard on every floor.

As he made his rounds of the factory, Jack found himself lingering near the places where the hands tended to gather to talk. He obscured himself around corners, in the spaces beneath the flights of stairs, behind stacked crates of products and parts, on the off-chance he might catch a guilty word. Jack recognised his paranoia, but in the absence of any facts other than the voice itself, there was no clear path to the truth. This pleased him, in a way. Uncovering an explanation would have undermined the homely fantasy that had provided him with a contentment greater than any one-night indulgence had been able to offer in a long time. In his heart, Jack didn't hope to discover the culprit of a hoax amongst the hands. Instead, he hoped to persuade himself that no such culprit existed.

The idea stayed with Jack—most often as he ate his meals alone at home, or during his walks to and from the factory—that the voice really was being transmitted from the future. A future in which men like Jack were free of the repercussions that held them below the waterline of their own time. Was it completely implausible that the device the voice claimed to possess was genuine? Even during Jack's few decades on earth, new concepts and technologies had radically changed the ways in which people understood and interacted with the fabric of reality. Sir Ernest Rutherford had devised a new type of radio receiver and then split the atom and touched the ghost of matter. Capital Radios was a figure in this march of progress too—manufacturing small marvels, each of them overseen by Jack. Why not say that a machine capable of sending a person, or at least their voice, into the past—into Jack's present—would eventually, inevitably, arrive?

Whatever the truth, Jack mentioned the voice to nobody. It was another secret he kept locked inside his ribcage, fitted neatly against the other secret he'd kept for half his life.

In response to Merchant's impatient enquiries late in the week, Jack assured him that the issue would be resolved before customer orders were due to be fulfilled. There was no concern about the quality of the technology or the engineering, and production was all on track. Jack added that he was sure he would find his answers here, in the earthly realm. But by the time Friday evening arrived—a full week and one day since Gregory's incident—Jack was no closer to resolving the mystery. At shutdown, he again sent his leading hands off to the Open Arms without him. He told them—lying before he even knew he was doing it—that he was determined to reach a firm conclusion. He would at least, he thought, find some way to convince Gregory that his life was not at risk, to encourage the boy back to health.

I think we're nearly set . . . Don't worry. You'll see me again soon, Ash. You'll hardly notice that I'm gone.

A sudden burst of static fizzed from the radio. The console hadn't done this before. It was always Jack who, each night, infatuated but exhausted, had turned the volume knob counterclockwise until the console slid into silence. Now, it was the voice that turned away, replaced by that rough and nugatory noise. Jack reached for the tuning knob and sent the needle searching—back and forth, back and forth, back and forth—but the signal was lost. The impassable distance between Jack and that familiar voice grew somehow greater. Jack had the sense of a long and narrow bridge collapsing, of a dream dematerialising. The voice's sudden withdrawal caused Jack to feel acutely his own incapacity to communicate, to reach out and respond through the radio itself. Of course, he could jury-rig the radio's speaker to act as a microphone, but there would still be no ability to transmit . . . And who would he be transmitting to? For all the references the voice had made to Jack's reality—though these had in fact been few compared to the wealth of other, daily matters—in the end, it was just another unreal sound pouring out of the ether. A spectral quavering of pitch and volume, machine parts and air resonating, mimicking life. In truth, it was a dead voice, like any other that spilled from the radio, even if a living human being was at its source.

Jack sat gazing at the carved details of the radio's cabinetry, at the shapes inside the orchestra pit positioned beneath the rise of the stage, in which slits of grill cloth concealed the twin speakers. At the stage's broad arch, bordered along its top and sides with folds of gathering drapes. At the bright emerald frequency band, embedded and backlit behind glass, hovering above all like a divine catwalk. No human figures occupied the stage, though Jack had imagined people moving in the wood's flowing grain.

Jack shifted his gaze and peered with his mind's eye beyond the console's ornate exterior. He envisaged the guts of the machine. Not the internal components as he knew them to be, but as the men and women of the factory perhaps imagined they had become—and perhaps as they really were. He saw clouds of a sickly green smoke veined with bolts of orange lightning. He saw a small demon perched on a stool the same as his. The demon's fiery, double-horned face stared at Jack from the space beyond the portal of the carved stage. Its leathery, ophidian lips, from which had surely spilled the words that held Jack captive, were now pursed in a smirk behind a bulbous microphone.

Jack switched the radio off. The static ceased and the emerald backlight of the frequency band dimmed and went out. In his mind, he replayed the radio's last words: *You'll hardly notice that I'm gone.* Jack stood and tugged the chain that controlled the room's bare bulb. The light slowly burned down, and as darkness filled the room, the abstracted shapes of the shelves stacked with Peter's traded radios—mostly kitchen-table receivers—reminded Jack of the irregular stones of a castle's walls.

Then, his eyesight adjusting, Jack noticed against the rigid pattern of the rear shelves the organic silhouette of a man.

'Is someone there?' that dark form said.

Jack moaned and sat heavily on the stool as the last threads of light vanished from his sight, and he toppled backwards.

The sound of the radio played in Jack's ear. *You're all right, you're all right. I didn't mean to scare you. I didn't mean for this to happen at all.* Jack felt a radiant warmth against his face and neck. A comforting embrace around his chest. Amber light shone brightly in the few patches where his vision wasn't obscured. He was being lifted, propped to sit upright against the door. The embrace loosened and, as the warm body withdrew, light again filled Jack's eyes. A man was sitting before him.

'It's chilly in here. Are you cold?' the man said, his voice a perfect match to the one from the radio.

Jack nodded and the man looked around. He saw the sheet on the ground that Peter had used to cover the console, and then he eyed the shelves. He rose, picked up another sheet from a small stack, unfolded it and wrapped it around Jack. It was enough to slow Jack's shivering.

The man sat down. 'How's the head?'

'You're not the demon I was beginning to imagine,' Jack said.

'A demon? No, I'm just an ordinary man.'

'An ordinary man can't do what you've done.' Jack's head throbbed.

'I'm not going to hurt you,' the man said. 'But we should address this situation.'

'Yes . . . How did you get in here?'

'A tricky question.'

Jack noticed a long scar running at an angle down the man's forearm. He wondered at it, but did not feel threatened. There was something detached but sympathetic about him, like a houselight burning in a distant window.

'Are we the only ones here?' the man asked.

'Yes.'

The man stood and, keeping an eye on Jack, checked the room, poking into the corners, cocking his ear for sounds. He had something fitted against his back, strapped across one shoulder. It was cylindrical with a taper at the top, made of polished metal.

'What year is this?' the man said. 'I don't see a newspaper or calendar handy.'

'The year?' The fog in Jack's head was clearing, though the throbbing maintained a slow beat. '1939.'

'Great. Thank you.'

'I recognise your voice,' Jack said, as the man sat down again.

'Sorry?'

'You were on the radio.'

The man ran his eyes along the shelves, and Jack pointed at the prototype. The man briefly looked back at the Home Theatre console.

'It's a beaut,' the man said. 'You're going to make a killing out of those.'

'A killing?' Jack noted the alarm in his own voice.

'A fortune, I mean. You heard me speaking through that?'

'A few things.'

'What things?'

Jack considered everything he had heard and the one thing he hadn't. 'You spoke of Gregory's death.'

'Gregory.' The man paused. 'He's a young guy, working here in the factory?'

Jack said nothing.

'Last name of Ford, is that right?'

'Yes.' Perhaps this man knew everything already. At least, there seemed to be little point in maintaining denials. 'You scared him terribly. He's been off work the whole week since.'

'I haven't been feeling too good myself. Do you know if anybody else heard me saying things—over the radio?'

'A handful of people, only regarding Gregory.'

The man stared down at Jack. 'Uh-huh.'

'I shut the radio away in here afterwards. There's another console, but it's not wired.'

'It's only yourself who's been listening, otherwise?'

'People thought you were a phantom of some kind.'

'Is that so? Maybe we should let them keep thinking as much.' The man pivoted around on the stool, his back to Jack. He ran a hand over the console's top, then across the shaped details on the front of the cabinetry. 'It's a nice piece of craftwork. Curious that you heard me through it.' He turned to face Jack again. 'Sorry. I haven't introduced myself—I'm Dylan.'

The man named Dylan reached out an open hand. Jack looked from his hand to his face. His features were kind, handsome. They bore the complex signatures of a mixed heritage. Yet, the bright green of the man's eyes reminded Jack of Dot—and of Gregory.

Jack brought his hand up to shake Dylan's. 'Jack.'

'What do you do here in the radio factory, Jack?'

'I'm the foreman.'

'A responsible position. You keep the place ticking over pretty well?'

'If the workers are happy, the work gets done.'

'Gregory's a good worker?'

'Yes.'

'You take good care of him?'

'He'll always have a place in the factory.'

'You know, I don't think I said Gregory would die.'

Jack paused. 'People heard you.'

'I'm sure they heard something.'

'They heard you speak of a dreadful incident—and a haunting. My workers aren't liars. Gregory's not a liar.'

'Misunderstandings happen more readily than they should . . . There was only a story I knew, about an encounter Gregory had with a ghost. Though I'm not superstitious myself.'

Jack and the man regarded one another.

Then the man smiled, and Jack said, 'You've really come from the future?'

'Did I say that?'

Jack shook his head. 'Not knowingly.'

'Hm.'

'Are there others who can—who can travel . . .'

'It's not like a taxi service, sorry.' He tapped his wrists. 'I have special technology inside me, in my blood. Your body has to be a part of the taxi, you see?'

The man unslung the object from around his shoulder. An ethereal blue light shone at the cylinder's base.

'It's been on the blink. I'd say, from the sounds of things, that there's been a causal loop.' The man gave the cylinder a tap with his finger. 'To prevent further leakages through time, I'll try to stop things up at my end. But as a bit of insurance, if you could do something about that radio, I'd rest much easier . . . Look, you can't breathe a word about any of this, okay? What you've heard over the radio, our time together tonight. I'm going to ignore the usual protocols here—they're unpleasant. Instead, I'd rather have you on my side, helping keep Gregory safe.'

'I hope to.'

The man frowned. 'Sorry, I have to check this with you,' he said. 'I have to make sure. Did you hear anything else broadcast over that radio? I appreciate your honesty.'

'Nothing much,' Jack said, and a flush of shame kept him quiet a few moments. 'Just you talking with someone, going about your business. In your home, I think. I couldn't hear the other person.'

As Jack spoke, the man didn't take his eyes off him. Then his features relaxed into a more open expression, a look of understanding.

'You tuned in regularly to that?' he said. 'To my home life?'

Jack nodded. He glanced again at the scar running pinkly along the man's forearm.

'Hm. Uh-huh,' the man said, as if deciding something. 'Ashton is the other bloke's name. He's a good man. Saved my skin more than once.'

'I gathered you care a great deal for each other. I found it interesting, and I . . . I liked hearing it. I wished I could talk back.'

'We do care, rather a lot . . . It really meant something to you, hearing that?'

'It did.'

'I'll be honest, the future's not all roses. But I think I can see why you might want to escape the present. I can't do that for you, and you absolutely must alter or—preferably—destroy this radio . . .' The man pressed a thoughtful finger to his lips. 'But if you feel like you want to connect again, try writing me a letter. Address it to Dylan—*Dear Dylan*—nothing tricky. Then store the letters somewhere safe and, when you feel ready, seal them in a box and bury it . . . maybe in the south-east corner of the factory grounds? I'll dig the box up when I get back, in the future, and I'll read everything you've put down. I'll read every word. Okay?'

Words flowing in one direction. Letters with no hope of a reply. Yet it was something, Jack reasoned. It was a chance for guiltless confession. A chance for true expression, a chance to be his real self. Would it not in fact be a new way of being, however slight, within a different kind of world, however remote in time? And although Jack and his audience would remain separated by that dark valley of time, hadn't they already been rescued from the fate of abstraction, from remaining always obscured behind the mask of the radio waves, of words inked upon a page? I will know his face, Jack thought, and he will know mine. He will hear me and see me, and he will know me.

'I will,' Jack said. 'Thank you.'

'Good. I look forward to reading them, to learning about a new friend, if I can say that. Now'—Dylan smiled at Jack again 'how about we chalk it up to a prank? Rather than a ghost, let people think it was all a put-on. Teenagers causing trouble. Steer away from any frightful notions, and restore Gregory's confidence.'

'You have a strong interest in Gregory's wellbeing.'

'We share a family lineage—he's several great-greats removed, but the connection's clear. It's important to me that he stays fit, healthy and alive.'

A stillness fell over them, and Jack felt a familiar melancholy stir in his chest. He'd said goodbye to enough people who he'd wanted to remain close to but never could. Having made it here safely once, might not this man, Dylan, manage it again?

A faint scratching penetrated the silence, coming from just beyond the storage room.

Both men stiffened.

Then Jack shuffled around to peer through a narrow gap between two boards of the door. The splinters of light that escaped the room were not enough to dispel the dark. He stood and gathered his sheet about him, but already Dylan had tugged the slender chain for the overhead bulb. As the light faded, Dylan retreated carefully past the console to the rear of the room. Jack felt for the door and eased it open. Still draped in his sheet, he stumbled out into the corridor, groaning as he tripped over the box of chains, spilling them in a dull rattle across the floor.

There came more scratching from nearby.

'Who is it?' Jack said.

Something tugged on the edge of Jack's sheet where it trailed behind him. He turned and saw dimly against the pale fabric the figure of a large rat scurrying away.

Jack sighed and returned to the storage room. 'It was nothing,' he announced into that darkened space. 'Nothing at all.' But there was no reply and Jack knew that he was already alone.

Being Neighbourly

I

PICK UP YOUR DOG POOP + 16 other top posts

Desperately seeking a handy person + 17 other top posts

Visiting black kitty – does it have a home? + 14 other top posts

Dubious characters lurking about + 10 other top posts

Adopt a streetlight! + 9 other top posts

Residential parking at an absolute premium + 12 other top posts

Physics Tutor needed + 19 other top posts

SERVICE UPDATE: What's hot in your area?

II

Boxer dog missing, answers to Rudolf + 11 other top posts

How to get mould off curtains + 13 other top posts

Cat burglar caught 'red pawed' with woolly items + 8 other top posts

STOLEN Sony 250GB HDD/DVD & Sony 32" LED Smart TV + 12 other top posts

Community planting day this weekend! + 10 other top posts

Non-residents parking in residential parks + 12 other top posts

Hit and Run – all witnesses sought + 17 other top posts

SERVICE UPDATE: Your neighbours are talking.

III

Return of Rudolf on owner's assurance to PICK UP POOP
+ 14 other top posts

On the scrounge for a fridge and oven + 19 other top posts

Meow! ('Sorry!') Rightful owners pls collect socks, gloves,
etc. + 10 other top posts

Robbed in broad daylight!! + 17 other top posts

Public Meeting – 3000sqm of green belt to be cleared! + 16
other top posts

Public meeting on bus stop relocation and extra parking +
20 other top posts

Have you seen this white customised Honda Civic? + 12
other top posts

SERVICE UPDATE: Want to win a luxurious getaway?

IV

Reliable dog walker/sitter needed ASAP + 17 other top posts

House painting help please + 19 other top posts

Anybody know this snooping pussycat? + 22 other top posts

Few things 4 sale – txt this number + 12 other top posts

Help clean up our dirty streets! + 9 other top posts

Inconsiderate parking and a very nasty response + 11 other
top posts

Funeral Notice – soccer star, budding scientist – all welcome
+ 15 other top posts

SERVICE UPDATE: It's a redraw! Are you a winner?

V

No judgement please, rehoming dog + 16 other top posts

Awesome 3 bedroom rental available immediately + 7 other
top posts

Dead black cat + 8 other top posts

Important – urgent scam alert + 14 other top posts

Do you have ANY community spirit?! + 10 other top posts

Parking wardens hitting the streets :) + 8 other top posts

Free desk, physics text books, other study items + 21 other top posts

SERVICE UPDATE: Is everything all right in your area?

Blue Horse Overdrive[1]

By Jay Storm | guest writer

A certain energy surged through the people and swept through the long grass of the paddock, towards the ragged pine trees at the far boundary. Batty turned to me and twirled his finger, meaning, Let's capitalise on this immediately, no more crowd banter. I turned to Rāwiri behind the drums and he hit four on the snare and then I laid into the bass for 'Damage Control'. This was touching the dream we'd had for six years. There were faces in the crowd that none of us recognised, come all the way from who knew where. And they hadn't come simply for an open space to drop a tab or guzzle piss, either. They'd paid a fiver each to get in, and Batty's old man was keeping crowd control with his mates— which was fair enough, it being his paddock, his property. I saw Batty's old man punch one of his mates in the arm and point up at the makeshift stage like, That's my kid, would you listen to those lungs, that crazy guitar! Our music wasn't his shot of liquor. Too much overdrive, like a fucked-up weed-whacker—his words. But there he was, punching his mate's arm, grinning like hell and bobbing his head, though struggling to maintain the beat.

---

1   First published online in the Capital Records Story for a Song series, offering first-hand insights into the origins of great Kiwi music from the label's catalogue.

Having felt that energy discharge through their ranks, the crowd leapt and tore up the grass. I was goading them with a look that said, Go on, enjoy yourselves, you wonderful punks! I didn't need to look down. I can play bass totally blind, my fingers moving across the strings according to internalised patterns stored in some deep part of my brainmeat. I also write most of our songs, so they're a part of me right from the get-go.

I scanned the entire crowd, trying to connect with every punk in the paddock, even those whose faces were cast in shadow by the dusk light. Where the half-dozen pine trees marked the far boundary of the paddock, I saw something like a piece of the sky move. It shimmered between the tree trunks. Its form was vaporous in the darkening evening, its motion flawless and fluid. It was a horse—a pale blue horse. It reached the end of the row of trees and then turned sharply, cantering back the way it had come. As it moved, its smudged form became gradually more defined until its lines were crisp, its musculature visible despite the distance between us. Then it stopped and oriented its body towards me. Its eyeline cut through the trees, across the overgrown paddock, through the perimeter formed by Batty's old man and his mates, through the jostling crowd of punks, and then entered my skull, warming the flesh of my forehead and the bone beneath.

Rāwiri said later that I dropped to the pallet boards of the stage with my hands still fumbling at the bass strings, hardly missing a note. He said I lay there making stupid strangled sounds, spit hanging from my lips. When I came round, Batty's old man's mouth was covering mine and his breath was flowing down my throat. Batty was standing over his old man's shoulder talking on his mobile, describing my condition to the ambo service. Rāwiri was out of sight but nearby, his voice in my ear saying, 'Far out—far out—you all right?'

Behind a curtain in A&E, the doctor tapped my knees with a tiny hammer, flashed a penlight in my eyes and worked her way through a list of other neurological checks.

'Nearly forgot one,' she said. 'Put your arms out for me and touch your nose, left index finger, then right index finger.'

I scored full marks. My body did everything it was meant to do:

My legs gave a little kick.

My pupils shrank.

My fingers touched my nose, left index finger, then right index finger.

My et cetera did all the et cetera.

I was mildly dehydrated, so the doctor had me sip on a cup of enriched fluids, though that wasn't the problem.

'It's unclear exactly what the problem is,' the doctor said.

That was a problem in itself, she thought, so she wrote me a referral.

Rāwiri and Batty and Batty's old man were in the waiting room, waiting.

'What's up?' Rāwiri asked.

'Not sure,' I said. 'Could be anything. Could be sunstroke. Could be I'm stressed. Could be a tumour. The doctor doesn't know.'

'A tumour?'

'They're sending me to a neurologist.'

Batty's old man gave Batty a look and Batty said, 'You want to bunk at our place?'

I could tell they'd been talking while they waited.

'Nah. I'm good,' I said. 'I'm all right to go home. The doctor just said to take it easy, and not to drive, or drink too much.'

Rāwiri piped up. 'I could stay at yours?'

Batty said, 'Me too, after Rāwiri. We'll take turns.'

'Nah. I feel steady.'

The doctor had confessed she didn't know anything for sure. Her words were only words, pointing to no clear or immediate danger. I was still processing the day's events— the crowd we'd pulled, the weird horse, the collapsing—and I hadn't quite caught up to the part where I'd been given a neurological once-over at A&E. I didn't feel as though I was hanging off a cliff just yet.

My apartment consisted of a tiny living room and kitchen, with a door into a tinier bedroom and another door off that into an even tinier bathroom. Rāwiri was busting for a piss when I got up on Sunday morning. He said he didn't want to wake me, citing bad patient-care protocol. I said weeing on my couch was worse, so to just go ahead. I'm a heavy sleeper. He said it was a small relief, sharing a place with only me. He lived in a flat with four other people and only one bathroom. Three of them, including Rāwiri, worked in the movie business. Rāwiri did concept art—a skill we've drawn on a fair bit as a band—and although his time wasn't tapped on-demand as much as with the CGI people, he wasn't safe from regular bouts of long hours. He was out the door by dawn each weekday, to catch a bus near my place over to Miramar. He returned to his flat, much closer to the movie magic suburb, on Wednesday, when Batty came to stay. Batty had already taken the letter from A&E into the Music Depot, where we both worked, explaining I needed the week off to recover. Unlike with Rāwiri, staying at my place meant it took Batty less time to get to work than usual, though our hours at the Music Depot were hardly demanding. We never had to rise before dawn, that's for sure.

On the following Saturday, the three of us hung out playing video games and working on a few songs—on acoustic, to save my neighbours getting ratty. I'd played Rāwiri a couple of new sketches when he was on nursing duty, and then played them for Batty, and it was good that weekend to all be in the same room, getting on with what we loved doing most.

I'd kept quiet all week about the blue horse. I told Batty and Rāwiri the same thing I'd told the A&E doctor, that my vision had blurred and I'd felt euphoric right before I dropped—and that was true. I couldn't explain the blue horse, the way it had seemed to manifest at the trembling edge of the wave of energy that rippled out from the stage. Not without sounding like I was half crazy—or maybe full crazy.

Rāwiri and Batty went back to their own places on Sunday evening, comforted by the knowledge I wasn't wasting away in bed or lying paralysed on the bathroom floor, or else going into fits and choking on my tongue or busting my head open in an alleyway somewhere.

Monday morning I was back on deck in my black Music Depot polo.

That weekend, a sizeable number of guitars had been brought in for cleaning and restringing, and it fell to me to service them. The boss reasoned it was low-stress work, although they needed to be sorted for collection by five o'clock, some by three o'clock. It's a basic chore that, if you own a guitar, you should learn to do yourself. It's a piece of piss. You're welcome to hand over your money to the Music Depot or wherever, but it's neither necessary nor entertaining work for the people doing the servicing. Notwithstanding that a guitar freshly buffed and strung with new life is always a pleasure to behold.

Late morning, my mobile rang and I told Batty, who was with me in the back room, that I didn't recognise the number.

It was someone from the hospital.

'Available to see the neurologist?' I said. 'My appointment's still two weeks away.'

'Another patient postponed. We're offering you their timeslot.'

'Any reason for asking me and, ah, not someone else?'

'You're just on the list, sir. I wouldn't read anything into it.'

'And that's this afternoon?'

Batty was at the door signalling in a big circular motion with his arm, and hissing—*psst, psst, psst.* The boss walked into the back room and Batty repeated the words 'this afternoon' to her.

'Am I available?' I said, tapping my head with a finger.

Batty nodded, then the boss nodded.

'Sure, sure,' I said into my mobile. The person on the other end gave me the time of the appointment. I said, 'Sure, sure,' again and hung up. 'A cancellation. I've been bumped up the list, but they said not to read anything into it.'

Batty said, 'Sure, sure,' then turned to the boss and said he'd finish cleaning and restringing the guitars.

Batty's old man drove the thirty minutes into town and took me to the hospital. 'You don't want to be mucking around with buses,' he said. 'And you don't want to be coughing up for taxis either, not on your wage.'

'Petrol's not cheap, though,' I said. Batty's old man was having some money problems. We'd tried offering some of the takings from our gigs—given we'd started holding them in his paddock—but he'd said no, he'd sort it out somehow.

'Thought I'd make the most of the trip and drop off some wood,' he said.

'You selling firewood in town now?'

'Mate of mine manages a petrol station. He's going to sell it for me without taking commission. Left him the spare trailer, stacked up pretty good. Should do all right.'

'Every buck counts.'

'It all adds up.'

I didn't feel as bad about getting a ride then, though I knew he'd have taken me to the hospital even without the firewood.

The people on the hospital's front desk gave us lengthy directions, which we misinterpreted a couple of times as we snaked our way through the sprawling, homogeneous architecture. But we wound up at the right place with a whole minute to spare. I entered the neurologist's office alone, while Batty's old man sat in the bright corridor, squinting at a glossy *Metro* magazine, which he thought was a laugh.

The neurologist was a middle-aged guy who'd been a GP for decades, he told me, though he'd been a fully-fledged specialist for a few months.

'How's that going?' I noticed dark orangy smears near one pocket of his lab coat. My guess was lasagne.

'Nothing to lose my job over,' he said with a dry laugh.

'A positive sign,' I said.

He invited me to sit on an examination table draped in white flannelette.

'An incident in a field, I understand?' he said as he sat behind his desk and leaned back in his chair. 'Tell me what happened.'

I told him about the fainting. He had his eyes closed while I spoke, and he kept them closed for a while after I'd finished speaking. I couldn't tell if he was awake or asleep. Then he sprang forwards in his chair and his eyes popped open. He reached into his desk drawer and took out a tiny hammer and a penlight, then proceeded to run through the same routine as the A&E doctor, with a few minor variations in playing style.

'All fairly normal,' he said, and returned to recline in his chair. A pad of paper and a pen sat idle on his desktop and I wondered if he'd begin taking notes at any point. 'Had any trouble with your vision—dark spots, bright spots, that type of thing?'

'Nah. Except—' I wondered if neurologists could make referrals to psychologists. The neurologist stared levelly at me, waiting for me to get on with it, to spit it out. 'Except I think I saw a horse.'

'A horse,' he said. 'There a few of those around up there, in the countryside?'

'I mean an imaginary horse. It was weird. It looked blue and shimmery.'

'Where precisely was this horse?'

'In the next paddock, trotting along behind some trees.'

'Did you have a clear view of it?'

'It was kind of far away, and there were the trees. I could see its muscles.'

'And it was blue?'

'And shimmery.'

He picked up the pen, tapped it twice on the pad of paper, then set it back down without a single drop of ink leaving the nib.

'Probably a trick of the twilight,' he said. 'You get that sometimes, don't you, in the open countryside. There's not a lot wrong that I can determine right now. I'll refer you for an EEG and that'll give us more information about what might be going on under the hood.'

'Yeah. Good,' I said. The words *what might be going on* reverberated in my skull, their echoes suggesting other meanings. Like, *maybe something terrible is going on.* Like, *maybe nothing at all is going on.* Like, *maybe something unknowable is going on.* That last option seemed worse than something terrible but knowable, which at least sounded fixable. Unless it was something knowable but terminal— but I didn't feel ill, did I? My guts were churning, but it wasn't a sign of sickness, only nerves. I felt basically healthy.

'Do I need to do anything?' I said. 'Or else not do anything?'

I was thinking of the music. We had songs to write, others to practise. We planned to hold another gig in a month. Batty's old man would need to organise his mates for crowd control, and we'd need to sort out event posters and online notices. Rāwiri was designing a fresh run of T-shirts to sell.

'A bit of common sense will see you through. Don't overexert yourself and don't drink too much alcohol.' The neurologist cocked his head. 'Best to steer clear of other substances as well.'

The same basic magazine selection was available outside the EEG technician's room the next week. Batty's old man settled down with a gossip rag featuring a celebrity

newsreader looking rich and delighted on the cover. Inside
the room, I was directed to sit in a low chair. It forced my
knees high into my field of vision, blocking my view of the
computer set-up opposite, unless I tipped my legs this way
or that. The technician attached electrodes to my skull and I
had the feeling that I was your classic lab rat.

'Got any cheese?' I joked.

'Lactose intolerant, alas,' the technician said.

He dropped himself into a standard office swivel chair
and hunched over the computer monitor, which presented
to him, he reported, various graphs relating to the electrical
patterns generated by my brain.

'Hmm,' he said.

'Ah-huh?' I asked.

'Hmm,' he repeated.

'Spot something interesting?'

'Hard to say. Perhaps something above your left temporal
lobe.'

'My left temporal lobe?'

'Nothing significant. But not nothing, either.'

'Not nothing?'

'Something,' the technician said. 'Perhaps.'

'Is the left temporal lobe prone to, ah, causing trouble?'

'Depends,' he said. 'Hallucinations, sometimes, typically
prefiguring temporal lobe epilepsy.'

'Right. Does that seem likely?' I pointed to the wires
sprouting from my head.

'EEGs don't always detect epilepsy. Have you noticed any
unusual smells or sights or sounds? Even something that may
seem ordinary in itself but doesn't fit with the present reality?'

The neurologist's dismissal repeated in my ear, right
down to his breathy manner of speaking. *Probably a trick*

*of the twilight. You get that sometimes, don't you, in the open
countryside.*

'Yeah,' I said. 'Nah.'

The technician sat in silence another minute, then stood
and detached the electrodes from my head. He advised that
I could expect a referral from my neurologist for an MRI
scan. It was the usual next step when the findings of an EEG
were inconclusive.

In the corridor, Batty's old man was engrossed in the
gossip rag. I coughed and he shut the magazine and slapped
it down on the pile.

'Everything all right?' he asked.

'Perhaps,' I said, raising my hands palms-up in the air
like, *who knows?*

'Perhaps yes or perhaps no?'

'Perhaps,' I said, jostling my hands up and down like,
who really knows anything?

Batty's old man frowned and planted his hands on his
thighs. 'They still don't know?'

'No. They still don't fucking know.'

Arrangement for acoustic guitar is the true litmus test of a
melody's quality, for any otherwise distortion-heavy song.
This is conventional wisdom that bears out in many cases.
However, there are important tonalities and aural textures that
can only be generated by bringing electronics into the mix.
Thus, Batty and Rāwiri and I planned to feed a handful of
acoustically crafted songs through racks of effects pedals and
launch them into the world via a modest stack of amplifiers.

We set up the pallets for the stage in Batty's old man's
paddock and hauled our equipment out there in his caged
trailer. There would be no crowd this time—it was only

us pissing around trying to work out our knitting and determine an appropriate palette of sonic treatments—but the stage kept everything off the damp ground. I got busy implementing a revised pedal arrangement inspired by a new song provisionally titled 'Outta Time, Outta Luck'. In the back of my mind, I'd dedicated the song to a guy upstairs in the apartment block—a writer who I sometimes drank with. He wrote stories about a bunch of us who lived in the block, so it seemed fitting that he should get a song in return. He reckoned he'd seen the future and it was extremely bleak. He'd said the time for change is now—each perpetual instance of now—because the future is constantly shaped by present action. We have nothing but the future and we can avoid or achieve anything, given enough time and enough will, he'd said, then trailed off with a series of caveats about the universal wave function which lost me—we'd been drinking for several hours—but the seed of the song had been planted. Because of this theme of time, I wanted to utilise a particular delay effect, and although that seemed almost too obvious, there was a section in the song's intro and bridge where it would probably fit. I locked a spanking new delay pedal into place in the signal chain. The arrangement felt spot on, like achieving a perfect Tetris play, and I wondered even then if 'Outta Time, Outta Luck' might end up being our best tune.

I was focused on the world only as it existed within arm's reach, resolutely ignoring the row of pine trees along the far side of the paddock. I hadn't been back to Batty's old man's place since the incident and my guts were giving me signals that I hoped to ignore, primarily by configuring and admiring that beautiful array of effects pedals and contemplating the sounds we were about to produce.

Batty's old man finished hooking us up to the generator he'd revamped a year or two earlier, and then he said to hold up, not to get too settled into position. He went away to his car and came back with an armload of old blankets and pillows, the stack so high he had to tilt his head sideways to see round it. He asked me to move aside, and then he and Batty and Rāwiri began arranging the soft materials around the place I'd occupy on the stage.

'Can't be too safe,' Batty's old man said. 'That thick head of yours is liable to crack those boards.' He laughed and walked off, then got into his car and headed back up the long driveway to his and Batty's house.

We ran through some drum patterns Rāwiri had devised, which Batty and I found our way into okay, improvising on guitar and bass. Then we took things song by song, blocking out the movements, noting down modifications to the arrangements, particular riffs, textures, et cetera. 'Outta Time, Outta Luck' was the third song we tackled. We ran it straight through a couple of times to find the rhythm and the places where it was most difficult to knit our sonic threads together. Batty skipped the vocals to focus on guitar. He liked to bark and howl out a vocal melody, to get the raw sense of a song, before committing the lyrics to memory. But before that, he liked to get the guitar part down solid.

We reduced the delay effect after the second run, all agreeing it was too disruptive to the energy of the piece, especially when applied to bass, even though the bassline served an essentially atmospheric function during the intro and bridge. By the fifth run-through everything was beginning to weave together, and Batty spat out his senseless vocal ululations. We each felt a familiar primal outpouring spill from our bodies, the music surging through us in a manner that shook the roots of our physical selves—which were these improbable clusters of atoms responding in the only way possible to a universe that demanded our obsolescence. My body became hot with the feeling of the music.

Building to the final movement of the song, my neck dampened with the slow pulsing of a breath which, twisting around at the waist, I observed was being expelled through the broad nostrils of the blue horse, standing upstage left, its iridescent muzzle poised a hand-span from my body. Rāwiri said later that my head was absorbed like a brick into mud as I struck the thick layer of pillows and blankets that they had all placed in a protective circle around me.

The upshot was that my MRI appointment took place the next day, after I'd spent the night in hospital under observation. Most of the observing was undertaken by me and Rāwiri and Batty observing the television in the ward's family lounge area, until visiting hours ended. As they were leaving, Batty said to me, 'Jay, mate. You feel all right, don't you?'

Rāwiri was looking at his sneakers, and they weren't very interesting.

'Up here?' I pointed to my head.

'Yeah,' Batty said.

'Yeah. Fine,' I said, and then I lied: 'I really think it's the heat.'

'Yeah?' Batty said.

'Water,' Rāwiri said. He raised his eyes to look at me, then at Batty. 'We should drink more water on stage. Just take half a minute between songs.'

'We already do,' Batty said.

'I said, more water.'

'Right,' Batty said. 'And maybe wear caps.'

'Well,' I said. 'They'll stick me in the machine tomorrow and if it doesn't malfunction and transport me to another universe or something, I'm sure we'll find out things are pretty much okay.'

Nobody said anything, so I added, 'Can't afford to lose a bass player as good as me.'

'Yeah. Bass players are completely indispensable,' Rāwiri said.

'Bit like drummers, eh?' said Batty.

'Even Queen replaced their singer, e hoa,' Rāwiri said.

'Yeah. Now they're more like a Queen covers band,' Batty said.

'All right,' I said. 'Let's agree we're all somehow indispensable.'

In the morning, after I'd showered and eaten my breakfast of spongy scrambled eggs on a slice of spongy toast, the nurse arrived. He handed me a plastic bag labelled with my details. He said the M in MRI stood for magnetic, so I'd need to place any removable bits of metal from my body into the bag. Otherwise, the machine would tear them out and the machine and I would both be screwed.

'Incredibly expensive and you'd not look so pretty,' he said, passing a hand in front of his face like a magician's gesture of revelation.

I took out my dimple piercings and my labret piercing and put them in the bag.

'No other piercings?' the nurse said. 'Do you need some privacy?'

'Nah.'

'No jewellery, body modification implants, pins or artificial bones, any metal of any kind, on or inside your person? Anything in your head or neck is a showstopper.'

'Nah.'

'Great. We'll need you to sign this declaration.'

Rāwiri and Batty returned around ten, with Batty's old man in tow. They accompanied me to the suite where the MRI scanner was housed like some diabolical machine in an old spy film. Another nurse showed us to a row of seats in the corridor.

'Won't be long,' she said.

A few minutes later, a blond woman stepped out of the room. Her face was thin and grey and she staggered like she was drunk. The nurse took her by the elbow and pointed her in the right direction, back along the corridor where the four of us had just come from. The woman seemed to be completely unaware of our presence as she shuffled past us. She had a hand cupped over her mouth and she was making a long, groaning noise like the sound of a single word — maybe 'no' or 'oh' — stretching out forever. I looked at her long enough to notice she wasn't crying. It was somehow worse that her eyes, rather than being tearful, were remote, glazed, as if a deep frost had come over them.

The four of us watched her go, then we looked at each other and hung our heads. I reasoned silently with myself that this couldn't have been the woman's first scan. This was her second or third, or sixth. They couldn't have told her the bad news right away, could they? Hers was nonetheless the face of knowing and it chilled my guts. I craned my neck to see if there was another doorway down the corridor that maybe led to an office for consultations. But the nurse's body blocked my line of sight as she came back out of the MRI room, moving towards us with a light, friendly smile on her lips.

The nurse asked Rāwiri and Batty and Batty's old man to stay in the corridor. Inside the room, she took my signed

declaration and asked again if I had any metal on my body
or in my pockets. Two technicians explained the procedure
and the nurse handed me a pair of flimsy plastic headphones.

'It gets noisy,' she said.

I lay down on a long, raised bench with a section down
the middle that would slide me into and out of the scanner,
which was a large mechanical donut, its central void being
the space into which my head would be plunged. They told
me to keep perfectly still for the duration of the scan or else
the images would be useless. To aid my compliance, rigid
plastic bracing nudged against my thighs and arms.

I'd never considered myself claustrophobic, but as I
was slid into the scanner—with the bright room gradually
displaced from my field of vision by the off-cream interior
of the scanner's casing, which was so near my face I almost
could have licked it—I decided each of us has at least
one secret fear buried inside us, just waiting for the right
opportunity to emerge.

I closed my eyes and focused on not moving my head, or
any part of my body, and tried to breathe slowly and evenly,
as they'd suggested, 'like meditation'.

'We're going to get underway,' a crackling voice said
through the headphones. 'The noises you'll hear are perfectly
normal.'

The sounds were varied and too rhythmic to be described
as noise. There was a languid mechanical sweeping, followed
by a deep buzzing like a faulty and amplified doorbell, its
circuit switching on and off, on and off, on and off, now
shifting down in pitch, sustained in a continuous assault.
Then came eight blasts from an evacuation siren, followed
by eight pounding beats like slowed-down machinegun
sound effects, then the cycle of siren blasts and machinegun

thuds repeating, repeating, repeating.

The sounds were brutal but precise and I thought about sampling them. Rāwiri already used a trigger pad in about half a dozen songs. But how would we make such a recording? You had to be inside the machine to really feel it—the sounds wouldn't be as powerful from the outside. Might a shotgun mic do the job? We could borrow one from the Music Depot. I recalled a scene from a Joy Division biopic, where this eccentric record producer lugs sensitive recording equipment through the English countryside, capturing the distant sounds of the stars.

The scanner died down, its harsh music silenced, and the voice in the headphones said we were done. They slid me out and uncoupled the various braces, their gestures loveless and unflinching, and I was returned to my friends for transportation home.

Batty took up nursing duty again and stayed through the week. I was off work but had promised to be in by Thursday. I spent my daylight hours noodling on the acoustic and trying to get ahead a few levels on *Red World War*. I pitched the idea of sampling the MRI scanner to Batty and he suggested reproducing the sounds from memory with a drum machine. Rāwiri brought his one round on Wednesday night.

I started by programming the machinegun thuds, adjusting the tempo and timbre of a kick drum, mixed with a sample of me slapping the outsides of my thighs to provide an organic overtone. I fired off a twenty-second blast and Rāwiri looked up from the laptop he had resting on his knees.

'Hold up,' he said.

'No good?'

'Look,' he said, turning his laptop around to show the screen. Our Bandcamp profile was displayed, specifically the private messaging inbox. Rāwiri maximised a window and lines of text expanded across the screen:

> *Hi guys! Been super digging the tracks on your*
> *page and the crowd-shot vids on YouTube. Killer*
> *stuff and you play excellently live! Saw one recent*
> *video where your bassist had a bit of a spill?*
> *Hope they're doing OK because I have a fantastic*
> *offer I'd like to discuss with you all . . . Hint: it*
> *involves a recording studio ;-) This is not a drill!*
>
> *Yours, Danny Irvine (Rep. of Capital Records)*

We'd put out a few CDs that we'd recorded and pressed ourselves, selling them at gigs, but we weren't signed to any labels—big or small. And Capital Records were massive even then, with a bunch of their bands getting regular distribution across Australasia, a couple even making it in the American and European markets. In the tiny living room of my apartment, our three churning imaginations blew out really big, really quickly.

'Wait. Search for him,' I said.

Rāwiri searched online for 'Danny Irvine, Capital Records'. Several consistent results came back, including pages on the official Capital Records website. The man was more than a representative—he was a producer. His mug shot showed him to be a bald white guy, probably in his forties, who favoured old Kiwi band T-shirts. He wore a big grin despite his wonky teeth. His goofy, heuristic digital profile endeared him to us—Danny, Danny Irvine, Record Producer.

'Could be a fake message?' Batty said. 'Like, someone faking us out?'

Rāwiri pointed to the two phone numbers Danny Irvine had left beneath his name in the private message. They matched his contact details on the Capital Records website.

'If it's fake, they want us to call the real person,' he said.

'We have to call,' Batty said. 'We have to, right?'

'We don't want to risk losing our edge, though,' I said. 'We already have CDs, gigs, the internet. What do we gain from this?'

'We can have more of all those things. A much bigger audience. We can reach thousands or millions more ears,' Batty said. 'Most bands signed to Capital Records keep their, you know, their essence intact.'

I didn't mind the sound of that—a bigger audience, a wider reach, essence intact.

Batty bobbed his head from side to side. 'There's the money, too.'

'We don't know what kind of cash they're offering,' Rāwiri said.

'Thinking about your old man?' I said.

'Only out of my share,' Batty said.

Rāwiri looked at me. I nodded, then he nodded.

'Let's see what kind of cash they're offering all of us,' Rāwiri said.

'Okay. But let's still play it cool,' Batty said. 'We'll call tomorrow, around lunchtime. Make him think we're not suckers, make him think maybe we've got other offers to consider.'

'Yeah,' Rawiri said. 'Lunchtime long enough to wait?'

'We don't want him to think we aren't interested, either,'
Batty said.

'We've all got work tomorrow,' I said. 'Let's call him now,
while we can all talk on speaker. We don't have any other
offers and there's not much point pretending we do. We'll
just . . . see what he has to say.'

The other two hardly needed the prompting, yet a silence
settled over us.

'The thing he said,' Batty said. 'About seeing you fall in
the video—'

'I'm fine,' I said. 'I mean, they didn't say when I'd get the
scan results. But it's been three days already, so it can't be
anything too terrible, eh?'

It was simple, Danny Irvine told us. We were terrific and
Capital Records wanted to sign us up. 'This is not a drill,' he
kept saying. He encouraged us to find legal representation,
but he said the contract was straightforward. He'd post a pro
forma copy for our initial inspection—what address should
he use?

We gave him mine. It felt like the natural solution, being
the locale where we were seated at the time. My bandmates
decided that my flat was now our official HQ. I wondered if
they felt rough about doubting my health. It was a fair doubt,
but asking for the contract to be sent to my address—band
HQ—felt like a goodwill gesture, a vote of confidence. We
were in this together, me and them, them and me. It was an
agreement to our indispensability, at least for the moment.

The contract arrived in my mail slot on Saturday, in a crisp
A4-sized envelope addressed to the band. Extracting it, I
discovered underneath it a smaller envelope addressed only

to me, with hospital branding. It was a letter summoning me to see my neurologist.

I phoned the hospital and got an appointment for Monday afternoon.

'That's quite prompt,' I said. 'Is it, ah, urgent?'

'I'm not sure, sorry, sir.'

'You work for the hospital, though?'

'Sir, I wouldn't read anything into it.'

Batty's old man drove me. Outside the neurologist's office, he didn't even glance at the magazines. We sat silently side by side in our chairs until the door opened and the neurologist invited me, somewhat gravely, to enter.

'Fingers crossed,' Batty's old man said, crossing the fingers of both hands, and I disappeared into the office.

I moved towards the flannelette-draped examination table, but the neurologist signalled for me to take a seat across from him at his desk. He lowered himself into his chair and reclined. I noticed a textured green smear on his collar and imagined an accident with a saag curry.

A few heavy seconds passed before he spoke.

'The radiologist and I have reviewed your scans. With a fellow your age, there shouldn't be any possibility of an issue, not a shadow of a shadow of a doubt, such as the EEG and your experiences suggest. Yet there appears to be nothing wrong that we can determine. The MRI results are clean.'

A pause

'Nothing?' I said.

'Nothing beyond your experiences.'

A feeling struck me that I at first took for disappointment. It was like several of my internal organs had suddenly vanished, creating a vacuum so that I slumped forwards in my seat and let out a loud huff. It was like stuffing up in the middle of a song and failing to recover quickly enough so that people wouldn't notice. Except there wasn't the accompanying shame. I realised the feeling was actually deep relief mixed with the frustration of insufficient closure. Naturally, I hadn't wanted the neurologist to confirm anything terrible, but I'd hoped for more of an answer, for a conclusion that made some sense of things.

The neurologist handed me one small white paper envelope and one large white plastic envelope. The first contained a written report confirming my results. The second contained sheets of film with the images the scanner had captured of the inside of my head.

He stood and extended his hand. Tucking my envelopes under one arm, I also stood, and he shook my hand with three robust jolts.

'Eat well, stay fit, don't abuse your system, and contact your GP right away if you feel like your wheels are coming off,' he said.

I went home and examined the sheets of film, pressing them one by one against the living room window for a backlight. If there was a problem, it was that the various things inside my head felt completely unrelatable. I couldn't recognise myself in them. In some views, my insides had the geometric sophistication of a kooky cartoon: fat coils of brain, bulging eyes on conical stems, vertebrae like bat wings. In other views: top-down slices of brain like a series of smashed butterflies. Or like a series of Rorschach inkblots in which I could see only smashed butterflies—definitely not a brain. Incredible that this sloppy mess could give rise to all the facets of my psyche.

Yet somewhere in there, weird synaptic sparks were flying.

I had a vision of strumming an unplugged electric guitar. The strings still vibrate, of course, but all you hear is a cold and empty twanging. It takes a spark to draw the real sound out and send it coursing through the coiled pickups, the signal chain—the compounding pedals imparting their sonic inflections—and then fire it through the amplifier and out into the world, where it vibrates through the subtle medium of the air we breathe before transferring back into the body, beating on tiny fleshy drums and bony hammers, spiralling through the coiled inner ear, reverting into an electrical signal interpretable by the shivering brainmeat inside the skull—but not only yours, because this is not a closed loop, there are other people listening, a whole throbbing crowd, their auditory nerves also quivering under the pressure generated by the strumming of strings—and here comes the next wave of sound, and the next wave, the next wave, the next wave.

The soul we now know is electrical and can be communicated with directly.

I slipped the sheets of MRI film back into their plastic envelope then shoved the envelope as far away as I could under my bed, to slowly gather dust in the dark.

I picked up my mobile.

'Contract arrived,' I said to Rāwiri.

'Wicked,' Rāwiri said. 'I'm sure there's still time.'

'Time?'

'You talked to Batty?'

'Not yet.'

'Call Batty.'

'Good news,' I said to Batty. 'Contract arrived.'

'Cool,' Batty said, flatly. 'Dad's put our place on the market.'

'Oh. Well, tell him to take it off.'

'How much money is the contract worth?'

I paused, then admitted, 'I don't know.' I hadn't looked at the contract at all. I flipped through it quickly. 'It says stuff about profit share with the label. I can't see anything about money upfront.'

'No advance?' I could hear the hurt in Batty's voice.

I began flipping back through the pages, rubbing the corners to check none had stuck together.

'No,' I said. Then, as two pages separated, 'Wait.'

'What?'

'I'm not sure what it means.'

'But there's something?'

'Yeah,' I said. 'I think so. It doesn't say how much.'

We already had a conversation booked for Thursday with Danny Irvine—what he'd demurely termed 'having coffee'—but I thought he wouldn't mind if I gave him a call before then. His mobile went to voicemail so I left a message asking him to please return the call. Then I headed out to meet Rāwiri and Batty for a few beers. Rāwiri and I were buying, commiserating with Batty over his and his old man's misfortunes. Being within sniffing distance of a paying contract was worth a drink as well, we said. Batty wasn't so convinced. We could all agree, though, that the cancellation—or postponement—of my personal doom was worth celebrating.

I was taking a piss when I felt my mobile vibrate in my pocket. Digging it out, I nearly dropped it in the urinal. Danny Irvine said that he hoped it wasn't too late to be calling me back. I said the timing was perfect, and then I blurted out the question about the money. I couldn't decide if his hesitation in naming a figure was part of the game.

Eventually he gave a range, but before hanging up, he managed to repeat four or five times that nothing he'd said constituted anything formal.

I went back into the bar and told Batty and Rāwiri what Danny Irvine had told me.

'You're flying low,' Rāwiri said.

I looked down and zipped myself up.

'Think we can ask for more?' Batty asked.

'Āe rā. He's got to expect us to,' Rāwiri said.

'Yeah,' I said. 'What if that's the limit, though?'

'We'll push him on Thursday,' Rāwiri said. 'He's just giving a range to make the larger number seem generous.'

'It might be enough anyway,' Batty said. 'To hold the wolves off.'

The news gave us fresh energy and we tried to carry on past midnight, but the bars were closing. When we begged for one final jug, the staff threw us a pathetic look and reminded us it was Monday before relenting. In return we helped them wipe down the tables and turn up the chairs, then they kicked us out onto the street. The simplest solution from there was to grab a taxi to my apartment for some bourbon-and-Kolas.

There's a way elation can expand your energies to cosmic proportions and then send them collapsing inwards, shrinking your ambitions for a good time to nil, knocking you flat in the process. This was our experience as soon as we arrived at my place, and Rāwiri and Batty made their poor camp on the fold-out couch in my living room. Sheets untucked and with cushions for pillows, they sprawled out in their T-shirts and underwear and were snoring deeply within minutes. Standing there in band HQ, watching their collapsed bodies, a stillness crystallised in my being, which perhaps was a sense of certainty that the present would continue to propel me towards the future for a long time yet, and that each of us truly was in some rare way indispensable.

A groaning sound woke me a few hours later. In the stuffy haze of sleep it took me ages to recognise my own name. Batty was calling me, then Rāwiri, their murmuring voices alternating like the call and response of two animals who knew only one raw sound between them. I stumbled out of my bedroom and into the living room.

The blue horse was standing at the foot of the couch. Rāwiri and Batty were backed away from it, wide-eyed, though there was hardly any space to move.

Taking in the full sight of it, the horse's flesh seemed not exactly non-material, but not quite solid either, as if the spaces between its composite particles were nearly discernible. The horse blew out a hot breath, whitely visible in the humid night air, expanding like smoke.

I shuffled forwards to stand beside Batty and Rāwiri.

'You guys can see it too,' I whispered.

'Couldn't miss a horse standing in the fucking living room,' Batty said.

'Well,' I said. 'No.'

I reached out and held my open hand above the horse's nostrils, then touched the velvety grey-blue flesh of its muzzle. With the back of his hand Batty stroked its broad cheek. Rāwiri hesitated but, seeing the horse respond with a gentle nudge to my and Batty's touch, he placed a hand under its chin, feeling the soft hollow there.

'It's really warm,' he said.

'You thought it'd be cold?' Batty said. 'It's a mammal.'

'I thought—I dunno,' Rāwiri said. 'It's fucking beautiful.'

'What's it doing in my apartment?' I said.

'Escaped from a float, maybe?' Rāwiri said.

'How'd it get inside?' Batty said.

As if in answer, the front door blew open and bounced off the doorstopper, then clicked shut in its frame.

The horse dipped its head and the three of us withdrew our hands. It pawed the carpet and looked towards the door, so I went over and opened it, then stepped back as the horse nickered and carefully picked its way across the room. Its glowing flanks brushed the doorframe as it passed through. We watched it saunter along the ground-floor corridor and exit out the double doors—which were pinned open—and into the night. A shiver crept from the nape of my neck, along the centre of my skull, into my forehead. I looked into the mystified faces of my bandmates, who stared back at me and at each other, all of us aware that we had seen the manifestation of something righteous.

Later, Rāwiri and Batty told me it was almost like a dream. Except that they could recall the moment perfectly, which never really happens with dreams. The details usually get fudged, as the inconvenient stimuli of the waking world impress themselves upon the brain. The three of us still discuss that moment in my apartment, in the hope we might gain a shared understanding of our experience. But it's impossible, because how do you begin to comprehend your own experience of such a thing, let alone express it in words to others?

The only way to capture the feeling is to play the song.

That's really the only way.

It's not been as big a hit as 'Outta Time, Outta Luck', which is still the top track from our two albums so far, in terms of radio airtime. But people love this song, especially

when we play it live. I imagine us forty years from now—
maybe playing a special gig for a small crowd, on a portable
stage in the paddock at Batty's old man's homestead, across
from the row of pine trees—still savouring the song's delivery
during the third encore, or something.

So listen up.

Here is that song.

Acknowledgements

For the invaluable insights and support generously given during the writing of this book, I am indebted and thankful to Antonia Bale, Debbie Burlingham, Nicole Colmar, Nigel Connell, Tim Corballis, Jo Davy, Mia Gaudin, Anahera Gildea, Duncan Graham, Kirsten Griffiths, Pauline Harris, Sharon Lam, Clare Moleta, Kevin Norton, Emily Perkins, Lynne Robertson, Maria Samuela, Frank Sinclair, Ian Wedde and Helen Young. For providing ideal growing conditions, thanks to the International Institute of Modern Letters. For the peace and quiet while I figured a few early things out, thanks to the New Zealand Pacific Studio. For the kind assistance, thank you to the New Zealand Indonesian Association. For the ample good faith, hard work and wise advice, thank you to the team at Te Herenga Waka University Press, especially Fergus Barrowman, Craig Gamble, Kirsten McDougall, and my brilliant editor, Jasmine Sargent. Thank you to Jonathan King for the magnificent cover, and to Ebony Lamb for the sharp portrait photography. Thank you to my friends and family, for everything. And above all, my love and gratitude to Paul, without whom none of these words would be possible.

'The Universe for Beginners' incorporates the following exhibition text from Space Place at Carter Observatory:

In Io was the potential for everything in the Universe.

And:

Ritual of retelling
Every time the creation story is retold, the Universe is brought forth from the void once more. There is no end to the story, because creation never stops becoming. There is always a new generation waiting to add the next lines to the story.

'Being Neighbourly' incorporates and adapts subject lines from email notifications received through the Neighbourly service.

The opening sentence of 'Blue Horse Overdrive' is an adaptation of the following line of poetry (author unknown at the time of writing):

At that moment a certain energy seemed to ripple among the people, to flash through the long grass in the vacant section across the road and in the poplars along the fence.

Versions of some of the stories in this collection first appeared elsewhere: 'Jobs for Dreamers' in *Turbine | Kapohau,* 2017; an excerpt from 'The Ether of 1939' on Radio New Zealand as 'Jack' (read by Alex Greig), 2018; 'Blue Horse Overdrive' in *Sport* 46, 2018; 'Journey to the Edge' in *Capital* magazine online, 2021. Thank you to the editors and publishers for your support.